In the
Funny Papers

In the Funny Papers

STORIES

Heather Ross Miller

UNIVERSITY OF MISSOURI PRESS
Columbia and London

Library of Congress Cataloging-in-Publication Data

Miller, Heather Ross, 1939–
    In the funny papers : stories / Heather Ross Miller.
        p.   cm.
    ISBN 0-8262-1031-7 (pbk. : alk. paper)
    1. Manners and customs—Fiction   I. Title.
PS3563.I38I5   1995
    813'.54—dc20   95-21678
                                                                        CIP

∞ This paper meets the requirements of the
American National Standard for Permanence of Paper
for Printed Library Materials, Z39.48, 1984.

Designer: Kristie Lee
Typesetter: BOOKCOMP
Printer and Binder: Thomson-Shore, Inc.
Typefaces: Caslon 224, Comic Strip, and Cooper Black

For acknowledgments, see page 155.

for

Barbara and Gene,

Betty and Griff,

Marcella and Glenn

and for the memory

of my father, Fred Ross,

my uncles, James Ross,

Peter Taylor

Other Books by Heather Ross Miller

Fiction

The Edge of the Woods

Tenants of the House

Gone a Hundred Miles

A Spiritual Divorce and Other Stories

Confessions of a Champeen Fire Baton Twirler

La jupe espagnole

Poetry

The Wind Southerly

Horse Horse, Tyger Tyger

Adam's First Wife

Hard Evidence

Friends and Assassins

Contents

Sparkle Plenty   *1*

My Spanish Skirt   *14*

Monette's Fingers   *27*

A.D.   *37*

Billy Goat   *50*

Tansy   *63*

A Sleeping Beauty   *71*

Old House   *79*

Infanticides   *88*

The Other Side of the World   *97*

Family Women   *114*

Constance   *126*

Easter Hunting   *134*

Popeye   *146*

In the
Funny Papers

SPARKLE PLENTY

1
In the Funny Papers

The daughter of B.O. Plenty and Gravel Gertie, she was a startling little creation, pink and smooth, deep double dimples, big eyes
and that long whitey-blond hair rippling down her back. She lived
in the funny papers but everywhere you went in the stores, there
was Sparkle Plenty multiplied, a big pink pile of dolls staring and
crying out from buttons hidden in their navels, buttons you could
mash hard. *Aawoooh!* she said, *Aawhooh!*

And everybody wanted Sparkle Plenty, everybody. Quint wanted
Sparkle Plenty, too. His mother said, no, he couldn't have Sparkle
Plenty, Sparkle Plenty was a baby doll, and didn't he know little
boys didn't play with baby dolls? Little boys played with guns. He
could have a gun.

"I want Sparkle Plenty and a gun," he growled. "I want Sparkle
Plenty and a gun, both, dammit."

"Don't you cuss at me," she slapped him across the mouth and
it bled.

Then his daddy, Mr. Finger, came in and slapped her across the
mouth and she cussed at him and Quint both. His mother was getting ready to run off to Norfolk with a sailor. Mr. Finger didn't know
that. Quint knew. He had to stay in the yard whenever the sailor
came. He stayed out there and watched the men on the golf course,
hoping they'd knock a ball into the yard and he could capture it.
Quint had a sock stuffed full of these prizes, some dinted, some
perfect, but all of them like little evil alligator eggs, he thought.
Wonderful alligator eggs that could hatch out alligators that obeyed
Quint and ate up his mother and the sailor in the house.

1

Quint took the funny papers to the bathroom and tore out the frames with Sparkle Plenty and her long whitey-blond hair. He was only eight years old, but he could tear paper with a startling precision.

Sparkle Plenty was gorgeous, he thought, though he didn't know a word like that. She took his breath. Not a baby. Not a doll. Not something just in the funny papers. She prompted Quint. He wanted Sparkle Plenty.

The colored frames garlanded his hands and left smudges on the sink. He loved the way Sparkle Plenty beckoned, almost winking at him. She opened the door and welcomed Quint to come live in the funny papers where they would live together forever and he'd shoot anybody anytime with his gun. Or sic the alligators on them.

2
Mr. Finger

Mr. Finger, about thirteen years after that, showed up one morning wearing a Black Watch sport coat. And the way he edged along the golf course across from her apartment amused the young woman, Brina. Because Brina had a Black Watch pleated skirt, knife pleats, each one ending sharply below her knees. She wore the skirt with a white button-down shirt, black ghillies and black tights, liking the way the ghillie laces hugged her ankles. But the green and black plaid with its occasional bluish threads struck Brina as sad, also durable.

The durability of the sadness and the faintly threatening sound of the name, *Black Watch,* added to the mystery of Mr. Finger, an old man mysterious only to Brina.

Mr. Finger lived by himself, as far back as she remembered, in an old two-story house near the golf course. She saw his house rising out of the early valley mists, the mists and the house both reflecting the deep emerald of the golf greens. An ugly house, the graying paint blistered up rough as alligator hides, the shingles buckling. But on those early mornings with the green mists, the house softened and took on an Oz quality. Mr. Finger could be the Wizard lifting off in a balloon, sailing over the long rows of quadraplexes, leaving the town of Badin, North Carolina, forever.

This made it all the more amusing for him to appear in a Black Watch sport coat. When Brina mentioned it, her mother, Frances Ann, scoffed, "Probably got it from the Salvation Army. Probably got a million dollars buried in that house, too. Crazy old coot."

Brina watched the milk make slow swirls in her coffee. They were using Carnation Evaporated Milk, pouring it right out of the can. The opener cut an arrowhead into the top. She and Frances Ann lived in an apartment exactly like every other apartment in Badin. Long row houses painted white or aluminum bronze with black trim and dull red tile roofs like pieces of Dentine chewing gum. Mr. Finger had the only real house in town.

"Who told you Mr. Finger was crazy?"

"Brina, honey," Frances Ann exhaled behind the newspaper, "shut up."

Brina rubbed at her wild whitey-blond hair, touched a finger to her skirt, deliberately seeking the static electricity's bite. She considered the things she already knew about Mr. Finger:

He carved little novelties out of wood, animals and shoes, mostly shoes, and never people. Brina could go into any apartment in Badin and find some of Mr. Finger's work on a coffee table or lined up on the what-not shelves. The little shoes were brogans with nails in the soles and loose laces and flapping tongues, and on either side, smooth knobs where a person's anklebone might have bulged out the old leather. Such a funny thing to do, Brina thought—to put those—the bulges, like a person's anklebone, like a person had just taken them off.

Brina would hold the little shoes in her hand and rub her fingers over the tongues and laces, over the anklebone knobs, and laugh. She couldn't help it. They were so clever and appealing, and so perfect. And then as she put the little wooden shoes back on the coffee table or the what-not shelves, Brina also felt a little eerie. As if she'd witnessed something dark, something a little angry and proud.

She shrugged off such thoughts this morning. The shoes were what everybody always said, *Just a pair of Mr. Finger's little wooden shoes. Ain't they cute? Look like somebody just sat down and took 'em off his feet and dropped 'em on the floor. Ain't they cute? Ain't they?*

But, "Why does he make those little wooden shoes?" she asked Frances Ann over the Carnation Evaporated Milk. Brina's white-blond hair licked up over her head, lush as a jungle. She wore an expensive perfume, Guerlain, from Ivey's in Charlotte where Frances Ann went once a month for dental treatments.

"Brina, honey," her mother rattled the newspaper again, "I don't give a good goddamn about Mr. Finger."

But Brina really couldn't help it, and this morning with the green mists rising over the golf course and Mr. Finger wearing that surprising Black Watch sport coat, she let herself get carried away watching him:

He shoves off the covers and puts his bare feet on the floor, shivering. He owns his house, his cold floor, his bare feet on it, a great big old two-story house on the edge of Badin, all his. Not one of those ugly apartments built by the aluminum-smelting company, those damn Yankees from Pittsburgh, coming down here and driving around in long black Buicks in high gear. People pestered him to death, *Sell that house, get you one of them apartments, live modern.*

Damn Yankees, damn fools, he cursed without exclamation, but a steady observation of the facts, *damn Yankees, damn fools.*

Brina grinned in her imaginings:

The cold floor is smooth and comforting to his bare feet. He shuffles to the kitchen, an old man but—and here Brina puzzled, corrected her fantasies, maybe he wasn't the old man she thought he was. Mr. Finger had left past lives, rich and glorious, dark and curious. Her fantasies amazed her:

He doesn't even know I exist, doesn't even know who I am, that I saw him on the edge of the golf course this morning, that I make up things in which I rescue him from blizzards, floods, and other disasters, break into his house with the Red Cross, tote him off to Carnation Evaporated Milk and my mother behind the newspaper.

She continued:

The Black Watch sport coat droops from the back of a leather chair, the leather scored in diamonds, the arms and legs carved with goose heads. Brina knows Frances Ann would call it a valuable antique, worth money, she might declare, and caress the rich leather, thumb the goose heads, their eyes and beaks, yes, worth money. Proves my point, she'd add, he wears that old coat from the Salvation Army, but he's got antiques locked up in the house. Crazy old coot.

Brina sipped her milky coffee, shut her eyes, feeling comforted and challenged in the same moment, *Crazy old coot. He's got secrets.*

But his wildest craziness, the old man's richest treasure, his biggest secret, is Quint.

3
Sandals

Frances Ann hates Quint.

He took Brina, her only child, to South Carolina and married her where Frances Ann didn't get to see it or have anything to do with it. She forgets Mr. Finger didn't get to see it either. She forgets Mr. Finger altogether. Quint, in her mind, is without a family.

Two things protect Brina and Quint. First, Brina isn't a little girl, but a woman with a will to go anywhere she likes with a man like Quint. Second, Quint has a job. He makes shoes. He holds Brina's bare foot and traces it on a piece of brown paper. His thumb slips just a little along the soft skin of her instep and Brina flinches, just a little.

Everything moves like a ballet, in watery slow motion, a dream.

Then he cuts the sole of a sandal and stitches on four white leather straps with buckles. And Brina has a pair of sandals, the most exotic ever to appear on anybody's feet in the whole town of Badin, and a perfect fit.

This was before they got married. And when Brina showed them to Frances Ann, she couldn't help bragging, "This pair of sandals I got on, Quint made. He's got his own shoe shop, and he made these for me."

Frances Ann was more impressed than she wanted to admit. "They got sandals in Penney's and Sears," she said, wanting to hurt Brina, to bruise her delight in Quint. "A pair of sandals are nothing but a pair of sandals."

"I know that," said Brina, "but these are Quint's."

Frances Ann hates Quint's skill. The right slant of the blade, the casual yet deliberate grip on the handle, then the slow hard push from his hand, a push that starts in Quint's shoulder and slides down through his thumb. An amazing ritual. Like the tracing of Brina's bare foot, the cutting of the leather sole and the stitching of those four white straps, these are things Quint can do that amaze and dismay Frances Ann. Things she can't fight.

And she understands why she hates Quint for his skill. Why she has to hate him. Brina is the dazzling surface, the easy display of this hate between them. Frances Ann wanted things like a debut at the country club, a college education, an all-white wedding. Then she wanted Brina to want them, too.

But Brina, taller than anybody else in this display, taller even than Quint, wants what *she* wants in a silent and determined way, the dimensions of which Frances Ann hasn't begun to suspect.

As a child she used to stand in the back door when Frances Ann snapped, "Get in this house right now. I'm a little annoyed this evening."

Frances Ann wanted to scare Brina then, but Brina knew it, and so had a power Frances Ann didn't have. Brina thought how awful that word was, *annoyed.* Sounding bland and neutered and yet poisonous. A boy named Noy Mull lived down their street. It gave

Brina the creeps, *Noy Mull,* like a white flatworm. Noy Mull played the clarinet in their school band and had big rusty freckles all over him. She made sure Noy Mull never got close enough to touch her, even accidentally.

And now when Frances Ann yelled and snapped and got annoyed, Brina did the same thing as with Noy Mull, made sure she never got close enough to touch her, even accidentally.

When Brina visits now, Frances Ann stands at the kitchen counter and beats up rich yellow batter for a cake, adding orange peel for zest. Brina watches, her brows lifted, "Why're you using a spoon? It'll take all day."

Frances Ann pokes her lips, "Your old mother-in-law up in Norfolk's got a Sunbeam Mix Master," then adds, sniffing at the spicy batter she pours into floured pans, "she got it for Christmas. Quint gave it to her."

"Is that what you want Quint to give you for Christmas?"

"Shut up," Frances Ann glares, "you don't know anything. Anybody who'd run off with Quint."

Brina pulls the rubber band out of her hair, gathers the long whitey-blond mass, fastens the band around it again, and smooths it over her shoulder. "Anybody who'd run off with Quint is me. And you can't do a thing about it."

4
Son

Quint does it all, carves wood to make those clever little shoes, and goes one step better than his old man, Mr. Finger. Quint cuts leather and sews it into real shoes that people can wear. He likes the pull of the hides, the threads and lacings, the quick pleasant clunk of the grommet punch. He could sit all day in the shop, smelling that air spiced with leather, fingering the toes and heels, fitting a perfect shoe to a perfect foot.

He learned to do it in Norfolk where his mother took him after leaving Mr. Finger. Quint was eight years old when she left, pulling him out the door of the big old house in Badin, staggering with the weight of their suitcases. They rode the Carolina Trailways bus all the way to Norfolk and they lived with the sailor she loved better than Mr. Finger.

Quint held the sock full of alligator golf balls in his lap and dropped one in every terminal they came to, Hamlet, Raleigh, Portsmouth. They clunked to the oily wooden floors and rolled under the benches. He did it when his mother was in the rest room. He had an idea he'd find his way back by the golf balls. Or that they'd hatch out alligators that would then come find him in Norfolk, roaring and lashing their tails outside the house or wherever his mother and the sailor would stay.

Quint had two golf balls left when they got there and he lost those somewhere wandering over the naval base, then the boardwalks of Virginia Beach. He wasn't hurt much by the loss of Mr. Finger. His mother and the sailor tolerated him, which suited Quint, and ignored him, which suited Quint even better. After the divorce, which took two full years in those days, they got married. They never had any children. And on Quint's birthdays, they let him drink coffee and fire off the sailor's gun.

When he was eighteen, he learned how to make shoes. A few years later, he went back to North Carolina to find Mr. Finger in Badin. And watched him carve a few wooden things, then took the blade, finished off a pair of little brogans and set them beside the pair Mr. Finger had made. Mr. Finger stared awhile in silence.

Then, "You got it from me. Not from her."

Quint shrugged, "I didn't get nothing from you. I didn't get nothing from her. Anything I got, I got from myself."

Mr. Finger breathed calmly, then agreed, pleased, "Okay, Quint, whatever you say."

And they kept the agreement.

Quint likes making things for Brina, little drawstring pouches of dark blue leather with fringes, the spectacular white sandals, wooden novelties. He fashions them with intense concentration, almost with anger, and with specific instructions, *This goes around your ankle. This you pull tight. Don't get any of this wet. Real leather hates to get wet.*

He wants to instruct her, Brina, the tall girl from across the golf course, from the Badin apartments that all look exactly alike, long row houses with red tile roofs, this exquisite Brina he discovered in the Olympia Cafe one summer evening and kept with him ever since. Brina with the whitey-blond hair like Sparkle Plenty.

"You live in the funny papers," he'd said, sliding onto the green vinyl stool beside her. She was wearing a pink pique sundress off the shoulder.

Brina snuffled up the last of a cherry coke. Ice shavings stuck in the straw and she coughed, grinning, "Funny papers?"

Quint didn't grin. He looked serious and stark, a big hulk of a person, but not as tall as Brina, young and intense, and silly, too, she thought. "You never heard of Sparkle Plenty," he mocked her. "You never read the funny papers."

Brina drained the cherry coke, eyed him, and put both hands on the counter. "I don't know you. Who do you think you are?"

Quint smiled for the first time, covered her hands with his.

They spent two weeks at Myrtle Beach, then Brina moved into the big old house across the golf course. Her mother hated it. Mr. Finger said, "Y'all can live in the house with me, I don't care." He shook Quint's hand.

But Frances Ann warned, "Don't you come crying back here. You made your bed, now lie in it."

But Brina did go back. Went back a lot to Frances Ann, not crying, either, but exulting in the things she and Quint did, sharing, she thought, the big old house and its surprises with Frances Ann.

Brina walked through Mr. Finger's house at first and blinked at everything she found, not the glorious treasures she'd imagined, but many rooms and windows and a brilliant oval of stained glass in the front door. It was a cluttered old place. Mr. Finger and Quint didn't keep it nice. Not dirty exactly, but overrun with their stuff.

Brina gathered some sheets, Quint's jeans, and some black wrinkled things that were Mr. Finger's socks, into a pile in the middle of the kitchen floor. She sat on the floor staring at them. Quint wandered in, "What you doing?"

"Fixing to wash." Brina flicked her hair over a shoulder and shivered at the long dry switch of it. She was bare-shouldered, wearing again the pink pique sundress Frances Ann made. She sat remembering the big deal Frances Ann made over that dress, *Pink pique, the best cotton in the world. I'm making this for you, Brina, to show off your tan. It'll look good with your tan.*

And she threaded the machine with 100% mercerized thread the same pink as the pique and stitched the whole creation together, a perfect fit. And then Brina went downtown to the Olympia Cafe wearing the sundress and met Quint. And after that Quint made the white sandals, another perfect fit. And after that, they went to Myrtle Beach and came back and she moved in here with him and Mr. Finger, a married woman.

Brina's whole life moved into a perfect fit. She felt squeezed into place by Quint's adoring her all the time, by Frances Ann's bitterness, by Mr. Finger's benign indifference.

"I don't know why I'm doing this," she said, separating the laundry into coloreds and whites.

Quint watched awhile. "You live in the funny papers," he reminded her.

5
Riding in the Car

Brina dreamed Quint died then came back to life and was driving the car. She couldn't tell if they were riding to Myrtle Beach, but the air was so dazzling bright, Quint's hands stood out like big fans on the wheel. Or big shells, tanned brown, the knuckles ridged hard. She liked Quint's hands, liked them all over her, or cupped around coffee, thumbing a cigarette. *Quint's hands are still sexy,* she admired, *sexy and strong. Quint can still take care of everything, make a pair of sandals, carve stuff. Quint's still got everything under control. And dead as a doornail, too.*

But who could tell exactly what was getting ready to happen with Quint. Brina liked that, too, his unpredictable moves, even in this dream—driving somewhere, she didn't know where, except she could smell the sharp salt ocean and hear it, too, over the roar of the car.

Where you going, Quint?

He shifted gears for reply, let his big right hand drop on her knee. And as Brina started to drop her hand on Quint's, she saw his hand was transparent. Saw all Quint's blood vessels pulsing like little glass vines, his muscles working, thick and clear as syrup pooling from a jar. And around their edges, she saw with terrible precision, Quint's fingernails deteriorating into a clear brown lace, the way leaves deteriorate in the fall.

Stop it, Quint, she ordered. *Stop this right now, let me out of the car.*

But Quint was driving the car straight ahead on purpose, until the sharp salt smell and the roar of the ocean filled up the car, flooded over Brina, swept her out and dragged her down with it. *Don't you kill me, Quint,* she kept at him. *Stop this right now, I said.*

It's you killing yourself, he smiled over the side of the car, down through the swirls and swells of water. *Just look.* He pointed his transparent finger. Brina settled to the dark bottom, glaring back up, both eyes the color of Coca Cola bottles. *You better come get me out of this, Quint, you better take me back home, don't leave me to die, Quint.*

You can't die, he said in a peculiar tone that both soothed and mocked her, *you're Sparkle Plenty, you live in the funny papers. Your daddy is B.O. Plenty and your mama is Gravel Gertie with pop eyes and peg teeth and hair as long as yours, except she's ugly and you're not ugly.*

Look, Quint, she started, *this isn't the funny papers. This is the car and you're driving us over the side of the Intra-coastal Waterway outside of Myrtle Beach in a rainstorm and killing us on purpose, Quint. And I said stop, dammit, Quint.*

Brina struggled away, the rain thrashing through the screens of their room and Quint's side of the bed wrinkled and empty. "I dreamed he died!" she exclaimed, "I dreamed Quint died and came back to life and tried to kill me in the car!"

Her feet smacked across the wooden floors to the living room where warm light glowed from the big glass lamps her mother envied. "Those are real antiques," Frances Ann pointed out, "hurricane lamps, Victorian."

A hurricane thrashed around outside now, the rain like whips while lightning and thunder exploded the dark summer sky. Quint hunched over the coffee table, white pine curling from his blade. She eased beside him.

"Quint," the fabric of the sofa pressed her bare legs, ridged her skin like braille, "Quint, I dreamed you drove the car off the Intracoastal Waterway and we died. On purpose."

Brina watched the white pine curl from his blade. Quint's hand never hesitated. The exclamations faded from her voice. She made flat indictments, then asked, "Why'd you do that, Quint? In my dream?"

"I didn't," he said, never looking up, keeping the blade steady. "You did. It was your dream. I didn't have nothing to do with it."

Overhead, devouring his sleep, Mr. Finger grunted and turned over. Brina thought how he must look up there, the chenille spread hanging off one side of his bed, big dust curls underneath and in the corners.

Big dust curls easing along the floor exactly like the white pine curls easing from Quint's blade. "I didn't do nothing," he included, "on purpose."

Brina smelled herself, her piquant blend of sweaty skin and the Guerlain daubed on her neck and both wrists. She made a point of daubing the Guerlain every night before bed, again every morning, and poured it into her tub bath after frothing the bubbles up to the rim. Quint liked to watch her in her tub bath. He sat on the floor and stared.

She decided she liked the way she smelled, sweaty from the bad dream, exotic from the Guerlain, and leaned against Quint, feeling the quickening of his muscles as he forced the knife along the pine. "Ah, Quint," she drank him in, "I dreamed I could see all the way down inside you. You were coming apart, Quint, in the water."

A growl, not unlike that from Mr. Finger overhead, stirred deep inside Quint. He still hadn't looked at her once. Quint's growl and his ignoring of her, gave Brina an immediate comfort. It signaled things were okay, things were under control. Quint wasn't impressed by her bad dream. Her bad dream faded just like the first exclamations in her voice.

Then, "Don't mess me up," he said, "I'm about finished with this."

He knocked the last of the shavings off the pine and smoothed it with a sandblock, blowing the dust, faint as his own breath, warm as Brina's perfume, across the coffee table. Then he took an oily rag and rubbed with precision, with love, almost with anger, until the wood glowed. "Looky."

A baby doll with big eyes stared back at Brina, pale hair in a long switch over its shoulder. "Sparkle Plenty," she acknowledged, and took it in hand, the oil mingling with her Guerlain. "I'll be damned, Sparkle Plenty."

"Turn it over," said Quint.

A long alligator tail, each horny plate perfectly cut, each husk and flake of the hide delicate as embroidery, stuck out of the baby doll's back.

"Quint, how come you put this ugly long tail on the back?"

He stood and stretched, pine curls tumbling from his sleeves, and went to the bathroom and shut the door. She could hear him tearing up paper and turning on the water with full force, snorting, gargling. And she had a curious vision of swamps, steam rising along thick shores, prehistoric pine trees dropping cones big as skulls, a fruity smell of resin and black mud and, mixed through it all, some mysterious irresistible musk.

This is true love, Brina congratulated herself, this is the true love of my whole life.

MY SPANISH SKIRT

Those days, I liked Dana Vann's mother, Janice, better than any other woman I knew in Badin. Facing a fresh six-inch January snowfall that kept us home from the fifth grade, she just shrugged and fixed herself a bourbon and Dr. Pepper highball. And while we rushed into the snow, rolling and sliding, getting ourselves sopping wet all morning, Dana Vann's mother heated up Campbell's soup. When she had the soup ready, she called out the door: "Sooooop. Good hot *sooooop,* Dana. Laramie."

I admired the goofy way she sang out soup, her voice going up just a little on the end of it.

We rolled and wallowed in the snow.

She called again, "Sooooop. Good hot *sooooop,* Dana. Laramie."

Again we didn't respond. So Dana Vann's mother hollered:

"Then stay out there and freeze your little asses," slammed the door and had another bourbon and Dr. Pepper highball.

I liked the way she did that. Janice Vann didn't mess around.

The next summer, 1949, we were supposed to be quarantined because of the polio epidemic. We sneaked and played together anyway, got hot and ate up all the Eskimo Pies Dana had in her refrigerator.

Her mother, smoking a cigarette at the kitchen table, observed, "You're going to get polio if you don't quit that."

Said Dana: "I don't care if I get polio."

"Shut up talking to your mother like that," said Janice Vann.

"Shut up yourself," said Dana Vann.

"Then I don't care if you get polio, either, confound it," declared her mother, stubbing the cigarette.

My mother always told me the three worst things you could say were: *I don't care, Shut up,* and *Confound it.* Dana and her mother said all three.

I admired them. They told truth with a vengeance and kept things straight.

Dana Vann's mother worked in Wiscassett Knitting Mill in Albemarle and had more money than my mother sitting home in Badin counting her Spode and Gorham.

My mother thought herself well off because she didn't have to work and especially because she owned Spode and Gorham. Her ambition was to own complete sets of china and sterling. A complete set of anything drove her crazy. She was never impressed by anything that was one of a kind.

Like the Spanish skirt.

Missing pieces, one-of-a-kind pieces, drove *me* crazy.

Like Dana Vann's daddy. Rudy Vann the Second. I saw some calling cards Janice Vann had printed up once: *Mrs. Rudy Vann II.* She put these things inside presents and sometimes left them stuck in doors if she went visiting and nobody was home. But I never saw the man.

Since we shared a duplex in Badin with common walls and sidewalks, six-over-six sash windows, and hip roofs with exposed rafters, it was obvious Janice Vann didn't have a man coming in and going out of her apartment.

I asked my mother where Dana Vann's daddy was. She turned to my daddy. "Where is Rudy Vann the Second?" She put a curious sarcastic accent on *the Second.*

My daddy growled. "Still in the navy. I don't know, dammit. Who in the shit cares where Rudy Vann the Second is?" He echoed the sarcastic accent.

I figured it was because my daddy was touchy and hateful about the navy or the army or about anything having to do with the Second World War. He hadn't been called up to fight and spent the whole thing staying with us in the Badin apartment, working at his job with Carolina Aluminum. He was glad of that. But he was also touchy and hateful.

I asked Dana Vann where her daddy was. She said, "Laramie, our husband left us," and went on throwing down jack rocks, bouncing the little red ball, and snatching up jack rocks before it bounced again.

Janice Vann called Rudy Vann our husband, too, and she called him a son of a bitch. I liked that a lot. Put the right flourish on him, polished his mystery until every surface shone. My daddy came in. He went out. He paid for my mother's silver spoons and china cups. He screamed and hollered *Goddammit.* He went to bed and snored through the common duplex walls. Nobody called him a son of a bitch.

When Dana Vann wanted expensive stuff, dancing lessons or ice skates, her mother said, "If our husband was alive, we could probably get that."

Their water heater burst and she said, "If our husband was alive, I wouldn't have to mess with this. But the son of a bitch is never here when he ought to be."

Dana Vann's daddy wasn't dead. But I understood the pure metaphor of their decision to talk about him as if he were, and it drove me all the more crazy. Their decision was as streamlined and natural as breathing in, breathing out. The son of a bitch was in the navy. Our husband left us, Laramie.

Janice Vann could have walked into Staton's Jewelry in Albemarle and bought a complete set of anything. She usually got the stuff Dana wanted, dancing lessons, the ice skates. She got the water heater fixed, too. And she underscored her efficiency with, "If our husband was still alive! But, Jesus, that son of a bitch!"

The Spanish skirt was mysterious and exciting and drove me just as crazy as did Dana Vann's missing daddy. Yards and yards of net, gauzy gold-red ruffles gathered into a sash, a good three inches of sequined hem dragging in the dirt. A Spanish dancer's skirt. A treasure Dana Vann yanked out of the back of her mother's closet, and then demanded that she give it to her and Janice Vann did.

"This is my Spanish skirt," announced Dana Vann. "My mother wore it to a dance. She had another thing to go with it, a thing you wrap around your shoulders and go out dancing."

Flounce. And gaudy promises. Such a wealth never appeared in the back of my mother's closet. I looked and found only her thick winter coat with mothballs in the pockets, my daddy's hound-stooth sports jacket that was too little for him, but which he refused to throw out. Blinking in the dim dusty closet, I fingered the rough disappointing brown and white weave of the sports jacket and I wanted Dana Vann's Spanish skirt. I wanted it as much as I wanted the rude bad things she and her mother said to each other, all that truth-telling and testifying that never got to see the light of day in my side of the duplex in Badin.

I wanted all the missing pieces to reassemble as dazzling as snow in my two hands and then deliver to me their secrets.

Where have you been all this time, Rudy Vann the Second? I would ask. What's it like in the navy? And I'd be flouncing my Spanish skirt, smoking my cigarette, clinking the ice in my bourbon and Dr. Pepper.

I'd steal Dana Vann's family.

It was better than rolling in the snow, better than Eskimo Pies.

"What have you got that skirt on out here in the yard for?" I scoffed at her the next day.

"I just want to fan around in it," said Dana. She knew I wanted the Spanish skirt. She fanned around, flouncing the gold-red stuff, hooking me.

"My mother wore this to a New Year's Eve dance. And at twelve o'clock, a parachute full of balloons fell out of the ceiling."

"How'd she get to go to a New Year's Eve dance?"

"Her sweetheart boyfriend took her. Our husband was her sweetheart boyfriend, stupid."

I never thought about Janice Vann and the son of a bitch being sweethearts. About Rudy Vann the Second's being somebody's boyfriend, about the two of them going to a New Year's Eve dance where balloons fell out of the ceiling in a parachute at twelve o'clock. I felt dizzy.

"Can I fan around in it, Dana?" I asked. "Can I put it on?"

Dana flipped her shoulder. "You have to be the boyfriend, first. You have to take me to the dance."

I didn't like being ordered around by Dana Vann, but it was her Spanish skirt and I wanted it. So I took Dana Vann to the New Year's Eve dance. We whirled and giggled and dipped and carried on the way we thought people did. The ruffled net brushed through my legs and the gold-red sequins slithered and sparkled around my feet.

After awhile I demanded, "Now, it's my turn."

Dana was leaning against the clothesline pole. She had a lobelia stem between her teeth like a cigarette. I waited as she inhaled, blew out long puffs. She narrowed her eyes.

"We have to kiss now," she said and threw down the lobelia stem, grinding it under her bare foot.

"Why?" I didn't want to kiss Dana Vann. She had green lobelia spit on her mouth.

"Because," she said. "That's what happens next. You take me home from the dance and we kiss."

Dana stuck out her chin. She looked stubborn, impossible. "Then you can wear it, Laramie. After we kiss."

I kissed Dana Vann. I rubbed the spit out of the corners of her mouth. I called her sweetheart. I said she was pretty.

"Now. I kissed you. Give me the skirt."

"Kiss me one more time, Laramie." Dana leaned against the clothesline pole and arched her back. She smiled winningly at me.

I kissed her one more time and Dana Vann slapped me hard.

"Why'd you do that!" I jerked back from Dana, feeling my cheek flame as red as the skirt.

"Because. That's what happens next, too." Dana stepped out of the skirt.

"Your turn."

My face burned. But my delight and greed in the skirt burned more and I wrapped myself up in Dana Vann's Spanish skirt and she took me to the New Year's Eve dance and I whirled and dipped in love with the swish of the net around me, yielding to the tease of the bright sequins.

At the end of the dance, I lit up a lobelia stem and stood puffing and staring at Dana Vann. Now she had to kiss me. Now I got to slap the shit out of her.

"I can kiss better than you, Laramie," she said, taking the lobelia stem out of my mouth, then locking both arms around me and grabbing me close to her.

Dana Vann plopped her mouth on mine, closed both eyes, flared her nostrils and pressed hard, all the time huffing and groaning.

I kept my eyes open. I felt my lips roll across my teeth. And I drew back my hand to knock Dana Vann across the backyard. If she thought her kissing was superior, I'd show her what gone-to-hell slapping felt like.

But Dana turned me loose and ran off before I could let her have it.

"I'm not playing anymore. I'm not playing anymore," she mocked.

"I'm not playing anymore, either. Shut up, Dana." I took off her Spanish skirt and let it sprawl in the dirt under the clothesline.

"Confound you, Dana Vann!"

That evening at dinner we had three full place settings of Gorham sterling in Rondo pattern and Spode Cowslip plates. But the glasses were the same thick shabby bargain stuff from Sears.

"That's the next thing we've got to get," observed my mother, ladling gravy over the rice and passing around the chicken. "We've got to get good crystal. Fostoria. I was in Staton's and I saw exactly what we want."

"We can't even get through one meal without her knocking over something and you want crystal." My daddy glowered from his end of the table.

"She'll be more careful with crystal," predicted my mother. "She won't knock over crystal."

"Shit." My daddy filled his mouth with food.

I watched him chew. His lips moved, poking in, poking out. I watched my mother chew. I visualized them plopping their chewing mouths on each other, closing their eyes, flaring their nostrils and pressing hard. I can kiss better than you, said my daddy, brushing rice out of the corners of my mother's mouth. And I can slap the shit out of you, said my mother, smacking each side of his face with a sterling silver spoon.

I got choked, giggled, choked worse and reached for my glass.

"What'd I tell you?" affirmed my daddy. "Can't get through one meal."

After dinner, the Cowslip and Rondo put away, we sat on our front porch, which had a pitched shed roof and was partitioned off from Dana Vann's porch by a thick tongue-and-groove wall. I sat in our porch swing, one bare toe skimming the floor, keeping a little rhythm going.

I asked, "Mother, did you ever go to a New Year's Eve dance with your boyfriend?"

I cut my eyes at my daddy. I hoped he'd join in, give me a grin, say stuff like, Sure. She went with me. I was her sweetheart. Her boyfriend.

He just unfolded *The Charlotte Observer*.

"Why are you asking?" My mother gave me a puzzled, though interested smile.

"Dana Vann's mother went to a New Year's Eve dance one time in a beautiful Spanish skirt. She told Dana. And she gave us the skirt to play with. Her sweetheart boyfriend took her to the dance."

"Rudy Vann never took anybody to a dance in his life." My daddy shifted in his rocker.

"I didn't say he took her." I stopped the swing with my toe. It held, waiting for the next little push. "I said her boyfriend."

"Janice Vann never had a boyfriend. Boyfriend, my sweet ass. She had Rudy Vann and Rudy Vann had her and that was it." He shook out the *Observer* and started to read again.

"Don't say stuff like that to Laramie," said my mother.

"What am I supposed to say to her?" he snapped. "I'm telling her the truth."

"Mother," I asked, not looking at him, squeezing him out of my brain, "did you go to a New Year's Eve dance where balloons fell out of a parachute from the ceiling at twelve o'clock?"

She considered me, then my daddy, then me again, and hardened. "No," she said. "I didn't."

On Saturday, Dana Vann was wearing the Spanish skirt around her head like a long gaudy wedding veil. It flared out heavy enough to pull her head back, all those ruffles and sequins rippling over her shoulders. I knew immediately how it would feel on me, the wonderful weight of it, pulling my head back, the itch of the net on my shoulders.

"Dana," I asked, "did your daddy really take your mother to a New Year's Eve dance?"

"I told you he did."

"Did she really wear that Spanish skirt?" I put a finger to one gold-red ruffle. "Did she, Dana?"

"I told you she did, Laramie. It was a dress-up dance. She dressed up like a Spanish dancer. In this skirt."

Dana Vann brushed my finger from the ruffle. "If you don't believe me, you can drop dead."

"What did your daddy dress up like?"

Dana frowned. "I don't know." She hesitated. "I don't care."

I moved closer. I moistened my finger and dotted a half-dozen bright sequins. "Where's your daddy, Dana? When's he coming back from the navy?"

Dana Vann frowned again. She arranged the skirt, covering up until only a wedge of her face showed. She pulled net across her face, just under her eyes. The net moved with her lips.

"Our husband left us, Laramie," she reminded me. "Shut up."

"You know what, Dana?" I pressed. "I don't believe you got a daddy. I don't believe he's in the navy."

"You know what, Laramie?" Dana Vann lifted her chin. "I don't care what you believe."

We stood awhile, defiant and self-righteous. Then Dana Vann grinned. "Today we're going to play bride and groom. I'm the bride and this is my veil."

She held the skirt out at her sides. It looked big as a tent. "And you're the groom."

"No, I'm not. I don't want to."

Dana turned around and around, the Spanish skirt sparkling, gold, red, gold, dazzle, dazzle.

"Shut up. You have to be the groom first. Then you can be the bride, Laramie. Then you can have the wedding veil."

She dropped the skirt and when it settled with a big swoosh around her legs, I was hypnotized. Hooked again. I wanted the skirt to settle around my legs with a big swoosh, gold, red, gold.

I married Dana Vann in the backyard. I kissed her under the clothesline and we paraded over the grass toward the garage.

"My turn," I said.

"No. You're so stupid, Laramie," scorned Dana. "Now we have to go in the garage and take off our clothes and fuck."

"*What?*" I dropped her hand. "What do you mean fuck?" It astonished me she could stand there and say that forbidden word and it made me angry, too. I wished I'd said it.

"That's what's next."

"I'm going to tell your mother, Dana Vann."

She outraged me. It *was* my turn.

"No. Laramie, look at me."

I looked and Dana turned around and around again, this time faster, this time with the Spanish skirt taking up air and billowing around her, flying like a big kite or a red sail, all its sequins catching the sun, around and around and around.

It was better than a parachute full of balloons.

Better than a New Year's Eve dance.

Better than a sweetheart boyfriend.

"Your turn to be the bride next." Dana Vann stopped short, waiting as the net settled around her, falling gracefully to the grass.

"Your turn to be the bride, Laramie, after we finish playing bride and groom all the way through. After we finish playing the honeymoon."

Something in the way she said *all the way through* alarmed me. Sort of sang it out the way her mother did *good hot sooooop.* But I wanted that Spanish skirt.

Dana glanced at her garage. "I dare you."

I wanted that Spanish skirt even more when she dared me. I wanted to spin around until I lifted off the ground and flew away, up over Badin, North Carolina, leaving Dana Vann behind, blinking. Blinking just like I had been blinking in the back of my mother's closet with nothing but a winter coat and an old houndstooth sports jacket.

We took off our clothes in the grimy garage. Dana posed in the thin light falling in long dusty bars through the garage window. She was buck naked except for the Spanish skirt, which she still wore like a wedding veil.

"This is the honeymoon, Laramie," she instructed me. "We have to lie down and fuck and kiss and stuff."

"I'm not lying down in here," I said. "It's dirty in here. I could get a splinter and a rat could run out of the coal pile and bite me. I'm not playing the honeymoon."

I drew myself up, buck naked as Dana Vann, and glared at her. Dana Vann ignored me. She smiled in a dreamy, goofy way and began flapping the skirt. She brought it together in front of her, the net swooshing in the coal grime. Then she pulled it open again, holding it out on either side of her.

Dana looked like a big glittering butterfly.

I squeezed my toes in the grime. "Shut up, Dana Vann."

"Come on, Laramie," she smiled. "Play."

I couldn't help myself. I dove into Dana Vann's opened arms, toward the glittering gold-red butterfly. And as I did, the garage door swung open and Dana Vann's mother stood there, a cigarette hanging from her mouth.

She stared at us and we stared back. She snatched the cigarette from her mouth.

"What're you kids doing in here?"

"We're playing," said Dana.

"The hell you are!" Janice Vann jerked us both by our arms. "Put your clothes back on. Right now, before I kill you."

She waited, smoking a fresh cigarette, while we dressed. And when we stood before her, clothed and uneasy, Janice Vann said, "Don't you let me catch you out here again. Don't you ever sneak in this garage again. Do you hear me, Dana?"

She took hold of Dana's arm and jerked her hard. "Dana?"

"Shut up. I hear you." Dana jerked back. The Spanish skirt was rimmed black along the hem, but its sequins still winked at me.

"You go straight home, Laramie," Janice Vann ordered. The smoke from her cigarette spiraled. "Your mother and daddy are going to hear from me."

I ran out of the garage, straight to my side of the duplex, up to my room where I sat puffing and raging on my bed. I was mad enough to kill Dana Vann. And kill her mother, too. They caused the whole thing.

I didn't care about taking off my clothes.

I didn't care that I played the honeymoon with Dana Vann in her garage and she said fuck. That we got caught by her mother.

I cared that I'd lost, for sure, the Spanish skirt. Lost Rudy Vann, the son of a bitch, the husband sweetheart boyfriend off in the navy. Lost the New Year's Eve dance, the balloons, the parachute.

Confound it. Shutupshutupshut up! I raged.

During dinner, the telephone rang. When my mother came back to the table, she said, "You can't play with Dana Vann anymore for awhile, Laramie. Her mother just insulted me on the telephone."

"What?" My daddy reached for the coleslaw.

"She said she caught them playing in her garage without any clothes on. She said Laramie probably started it. She asked me where Laramie got a notion like that?"

My mother looked at me hard.

"Well, where do you think she got a notion like that?" My daddy looked at me hard, too.

I looked into my Spode. The coleslaw straggled into a bunch of blue and red flowers. The Brown-n-Serve roll sweated against the fluted rim.

"She didn't get it from me, that's for sure," said my mother, looking hard at him.

"That's for sure, darling." He returned her hard look. "How could anybody get such a notion from you?"

"Maybe if you did something besides eat and sleep all the time?"

"Maybe if you did something besides talk about your goddamned dishes all the time?" My daddy picked up his Cowslip and threw it against the wall.

My mother sat with her hands on either side of her plate, rubbing the Gorham sterling. She watched the Spode crash to the floor, the food slide down the wall.

"You're just damned disgusting," she said.

"Don't ask me what you are," he said.

They didn't ask me a thing. Didn't ask me if it was my notion to play the honeymoon in Dana Vann's garage. My mother had been insulted on the telephone. My daddy had broken his china plate and now we were missing a complete place setting.

I sat there and examined the coal dirt under my fingernails. "I'm going to go take a bath," I announced. They never blinked an eye at me, just kept on staring at each other.

In the tub I scrubbed at the grime on my knees and between my toes. I gouged it from under my nails and swabbed it out of my ears. And all the time I assured myself that I wanted to keep on liking Dana Vann's mother, Janice, better than any other woman in Badin. I wanted to play with Dana Vann tomorrow and the next day, too. I wanted to keep on being part of their rude bad ways, sharing their husband, their son of a bitch, and their Spanish skirt.

I slid down in the water, my head against the white porcelain, and I fastened my brain on the Spanish skirt. My hands trailed the water on either side of my body, swooshing the suds gently, then faster, beating the water into froth.

"What're you doing in there? Drowning yourself?" My daddy knocked on the door.

I slumped deeper into the tub, only my nose and eyes remaining above water. There was no way they could get in.

"You've been in there long enough, Laramie!" shouted my mother. "Come out!"

I raised my head just a little. "This is my Spanish skirt," I told the water, gathering the suds around me.

"I wore it to a New Year's Eve dance and at twelve o'clock, a parachute full of balloons fell out of the ceiling."

I slung big piles of water up to the ceiling of the bathroom and laughed as they fell, splattering me, the floor, my mother's chenille robe hanging on the door and my daddy's splayed bedroom shoes.

The suds went everywhere. Better than a fresh January snowfall. Better than balloons. Better than a million gold-red sequins.

"There. You see that?" I addressed the chenille robe and the shoes. "That was my Spanish skirt."

I embraced what suds remained. Kissed them. "My son of a bitch sweetheart boyfriend gave it to me."

The suds spangled my nose and burst, leaving a faint sweet sting.

MONETTE'S FINGERS

Every afternoon Bev got off the school bus and asked Gage, "Is my mother happy or mad?"

It was the first thing Bev asked. And it made the worst kind of a difference. The events of Gage's day led up to Bev's one question. He put her on the bus in the morning as a thin white mist lifted out of the brush to shroud the Carolina pines. Then he followed his state park routine, answering mail, answering telephones, answering radios. And he met the bus bringing Bev home with the same question:

"Is my mother happy or mad?"

Gage wouldn't answer the question. But he waited for and dreaded it every afternoon, watching David chase the dumb friendly dog and throw sticks at the big park mailbox. The sun going down across the highway blushed Gage's face, turned the world bronze.

He dreaded Bev's question. He was ashamed.

Gage felt something slipping away from both him and Bev. It slipped away with a softness, like bare feet padding across a polished floor. It turned a corner, got gone quick. Truly gone.

The whole thing made Gage homesick and dopey. There was nothing he could do. The clumsy school bus chugged toward him and David. Its red signals flashed, the STOP sign swung out, and the bus reminded Gage of the old plow mules on his father's farm. He thought if he yelled "Gee, ha!" or "Whoa!," the old bus would obey.

Bev jumped down, her eyes solemn, dragging a plaid book satchel. She didn't smile or wave back at the kids screaming through the bus windows. She ran across the highway to Gage, catching her breath. "Is my mother happy or mad?"

He drowned her question with questions of his own, busy chattering: "Hey, sweetheart. Did you have a good day? What'd you get for lunch? Pizza?"

Gage met the solemn expression in Bev's eyes briefly, then blinked away. She knew what was going on. He took her plaid satchel and looked inside, calling, "Hey, David! Look what Bev did at school."

David came grinning, his face and hands grubby, ready to admire the crayon drawings, the flimsy pitched-roof houses with smoke spirals, birds like V's swooping off the page, goofy stick kids chasing goofy stick dogs.

"Daddy." Bev showed Gage a wrinkled page of numbers. "I didn't do no good. I got a bad check."

The 3's were turned backward so they resembled E's.

Gage folded the page. "It's okay."

Look, he wanted to soothe, the first grade's hard, Bev. You have to ride a bus. You have to stand in line. You eat pizza slices in a noisy cafeteria.

He blinked at her. The first grade is too goddamned hard for anybody. Making your 3's backward.

"It's okay," he said again. "Now, race you to the house!"

Gage clapped his hands and Bev and David broke into a wild run through the pines, "Can't catch me! Can't catch nothing!"

When he caught up to them, they were both sitting on the door steps with the panting dog, their faces red and proud. "We beat you, Daddy."

The children watched Ena all the time. She cried, raged, threw stuff. They watched. They waited for her to calm down. She had all the power in the family. No wonder Bev asked him, "Is my mother happy or mad?" Bev didn't want to be around Ena unless she was forewarned. And forewarned, Gage shrugged, was forearmed. Like the old cliché.

But, Gage tried to convince himself everyday, you don't have to explain this to a kid. Goddammit, he couldn't even explain it to himself.

Ena opened her arms and loved them one day, then shut herself up cold and hateful and silent the next. She was moody as hell. Unpredictable. Aggravating. He gritted his teeth. *Just once, I'd like to show her what she's like. Just once make her see it.*

Gage wouldn't bring himself to question Ena about what was going on between them, between her and the kids. That would be recognizing the dreadful problem. Giving it a name, maybe. Encouraging it to live out in the open. That would mean he had to do something.

He had no problem. He just shut up and hoped it would go away, whatever it was. Then things would go back like they were when he had brought them to the state park: Bev three, Ena pregnant with David, and Gage, proud of himself for getting out of the navy and Korea in one piece, was picking back up his civilian life so easily, it almost bothered him.

It did bother him. But Gage shoved it off. Rejoiced in all that he had. David born, they were a full American family. Nothing could spoil this.

David grew. Bev went to school. But in the splendor and isolation of the North Carolina state park, Ena changed. She said terrible things, threw plates, then withdrew into long awkward silences, coming out of them only to rage and throw more plates. *I hate you. I hope you die.*

Then after dreadful tears of penitence, sitting in the middle of the floor, kissing first Bev, then David, saying, "I didn't mean that. I'm sorry," Ena would swing back to overwhelming them with love, doing favors for everybody, picnics, stories, batches of cookies.

Then, days, weeks, months, maybe, later, in a split second, no forewarning, no forearming, she was back to her rages and her long silences, the bitter contempt.

And Bev was back to asking when he met the school bus, "Is my mother happy or mad?"

Gage was afraid if he answered Bev, the things that they all still shared, such as Ena on her good days, would dissolve like old-fashioned picture proofs in the hot sun. He couldn't risk the loss.

Supper was peaceful. Ena sat across the table from him and passed plates and laughed and listened. She charmed the two children and they turned their faces like bright lanterns, blinking, delighted.

Your mother is happy, Bev, he wanted to point out. To actually point at Ena and say, Look, Bev, she's happy. Keep this picture of her, Bev. Save it in your mind. Go back to it later.

In the night he touched Ena's shoulder. She turned from him, and just the stiffening of her back was enough to kill.

The puzzlement, the old dread and resentment reared like a stone wall. It won't last long, Bev. Save it in your mind. Go back to it later.

The next morning was cold and white. "This is the first frost," said Gage as they hurried out to meet the school bus.

"Oh, Daddy, I want it to snow!" declared Bev. "I want it to snow up to the roof!"

"I want it to snow, too!" mimicked David. "I want it to snow *over* the roof!"

The dog barked in circles, his breath clouding.

"It's not cold enough to snow," said Gage. "It has to be *cold.*" He exaggerated, wrapping his arms around himself and shivering. "It has to be *cold* as Christmas."

"*Cold* as Christmas!" Bev swung the book satchel, grinning. "Brrrr!" She shivered like Gage.

"*Cold* as Christmas!" David grabbed at her satchel.

The bus pulled up by the big mailbox and Bev ran to get aboard. "Bye! Be good! See you!" David and Gage waved her off.

Gage watched the bus until it rounded a curve in the road, then was gone. *Truly gone.* He shook his head, herded David back to the house. It was a good brisk fall morning. Ena would see how fine it was. Gage gritted his teeth, he would *make* her see. And he was surprised at himself.

But, he quickened his step, he would make Ena see, *too,* how things slipped away from you, rounding the curves in the road like Bev's school bus until they were gone forever.

Ena sat in the wing chair with a coffee mug. The scent of lemon-lilac softened the room. She was calm, smiling, the sunlight curling around her face and hair. It made Gage hesitate.

He was afraid of Ena.

He hated himself for that. Hated her.

He went ahead anyhow, chancing. "It's perfect for a hike," he said. "Down to the lake, what do you say? You and David and me?"

Ena gazed at Gage a moment and her eyes, big and green, so resoundingly green that they startled him, Ena's eyes were warm.

She lifted the mug. "I don't know."

David scattered a bag of plastic soldiers across the floor and began setting them up in battle formations. "Kpow! Kpow!" he shot them down.

Gage watched Ena curl a strand of hair over a finger, a habit she had. Curl it up tight, then slip the finger free.

"Look," he coaxed, "just try it. Come on."

The finger slipped from the tight curl. "Okay," she agreed.

It's okay, he marveled. I thought it was going to be bad. But it's okay.

Gage, Ena, and David, the dog frisking and scouting in the brush, walked spiritedly under the brisk blue sky. Leaves drifted through long chilly shafts of air between trees, hardwoods, and taller pines. As they walked, Gage indulged his favorite fantasy.

"This is all mine," he said, stretching out both arms. "Look, Ena, all these woods and the lake, everything, it's all mine. Four thousand acres of the best North Carolina parkland. And you know what?"

He dropped his arms. Ena grinned, snapped her fingers at David. "Daddy's bragging."

"You know what?" Gage repeated. "I'm giving it all to you, if you want it, sweetheart. All four thousand acres."

"This is all mine," mimicked David. He ran ahead, his arms like an airplane, the dog barking. "All mine!"

Ena rubbed her nose. "God, I'm freezing. Aren't you cold?" She blew on her hands. "I didn't bring my gloves."

Gage folded her hands in his, jammed them in his pocket. "Come on, let's walk faster to warm up. David!"

He motioned the child to hurry. David laughed, jammed his hands in his pockets, too, and skipped on. The dog barked at squirrels in the pines.

"Daddy, I can't run none with my hands in my pockets." David returned to them, stuck out his cold fists.

"We'll warm you up," said Gage and he took one fist and Ena took the other and they both rubbed David until he giggled.

Ena glanced overhead. "Look at all the grapevines up there. Look how high up they are."

"Who eats grapes way up there?" asked David. He tipped his head back so far, he collapsed, giggling more.

"Nobody," said Ena, tipping her head back, too.

Gage stopped rubbing David's fist. "That better?"

David nodded and ran on to the clearing he and Bev called The Secret Place. There a spillway from the lake fell in a glassy rush over a rock dam and filled the creek to its banks. Threads of bright water spangled the undergrowth. And as the dog nosed through thorn bushes, Gage noticed with a slight thrill thousands of drops clinging to the black sharp thorns, each one lit up by the sun. The unexpected beauty stung.

Four people were already in The Secret Place. A pregnant woman, a man with fishing gear, and two children like his and Ena's, an older girl and a younger boy.

"Oh, hell," said Ena. She resented park patrons.

"Calm down," said Gage.

The dog halted, raised a paw, and growled. The pregnant woman whistled, slapped her thigh, and he bounded over, wagging his tail, sniffing her shoes and fingers.

"Look at that damn dog," scoffed Ena. "A lot of good he'd be if they pulled a gun on us. They could kill us and he'd just wag his tail."

"Nothing would be any good if they pulled a gun on us," said Gage. "Calm down. They're just fishing."

The two children stared briefly at David, then went on with their play. They jabbed big sticks in the water and threw rocks as far as they could over the lake.

The man eyed Gage's uniform. "Is it legal to wet a hook here, mister?"

"Got a state license?"

"Yeah."

"I need to see it."

The man grinned and wiped the end of his nose with a sleeve. "Well, I ain't got it on me. Can't I just cast a little?"

His ingratiating giggle got on Gage's nerves. "Where're you from?" he asked. "What kind of bait are you using?"

The man hesitated. Gage said, "Look, if you're from Stanly County and if you're using natural bait, okay. You can fish in this lake without a license. That's all I'm asking."

The man giggled again. "We from over at Porters. You know where that is? Other side of Albemarle. I got shrimp. I use shrimp."

"Okay," Gage agreed. "But it's too cold to catch anything. Nothing's going to bite."

The man sobered, took on a proud look. "I bet you, mister, I can get a bite. I bet you, mister, if they's a fish in that water, I'll catch it."

He thumped his chest and bent to search his tackle, then stood up irritably.

"Ain't we got no more shrimp? Why ain't you told me the shrimp is gone?" he snapped at the woman.

"You know I can't fish without no shrimp. Now I ain't got no damn bait." He kicked the tackle.

The pregnant woman's pale hair, pulled back from a smooth forehead, dangled to her waist. She fixed her dark button eyes on Ena, scanned her up and down. Then, still patting the dog, said out of her pink mouth, tight as a bud, not even looking at the man, but straight at Gage as if to measure the effect on him alone:

"Use one of Monette's fingers."

The little girl stopped playing and stared at her mother, then her father, then Gage, Ena, and David. Her button eyes were as dark as her mother's, her forehead as smooth, and her long hair as pale. But her pink lips were not tight. Monette's pink lips poked out full, then parted over her small hard teeth.

"Whaaat?" she drawled.

The woman scratched the dog's ears. "I said 'use one of Monette's fingers.'" Without the slightest hint of a joke. No giggle. Just a straight cold-blooded fact.

Use one of Monette's fingers.

Gage blinked when he heard that. He knew the child heard it right the first time. Monette's face wavered a moment between terror and surprise, then hardened to definite defiance.

"You just try," she said and fisted both hands.

Gage stepped back to grab the cold hands of both David and Ena. He stood between them, squeezing their hands, jamming their hands into the pockets on either side of his jacket.

The pregnant woman snickered.

In a quick sickening vision, Gage saw the finger barbed on the hook, the hook flashing over the water, sinking, the finger darkening under water, then struck, bitten, swallowed by a fish.

He started to say something, almost believing his fantasy, when the woman jumped up, scolding, "Clifford! Clifford!"

The little boy was crawling out on the rock dam, slapping at the hard rushing water with his stick.

"Clifford," continued the woman, "that water looks mighty cold. Get back from there, Clifford. That man don't want to have to pull you out."

The dog rolled at her feet. She put a navy blue Ked tenderly on his belly, pressed until he groaned with delight, and still scolded the boy on the dam.

"I don't want to have to make that man pull you out, Clifford," she repeated. She looked hard at Gage, then at Ena, and finally at David. She looked as if she expected them all three to strip and plunge into the cold water immediately.

Ena dropped Gage's hand, took a step. "I hate you," she said to the pregnant woman. "I hope you die."

The woman took her foot off the dog, gazed a moment at Ena. Gage felt paralyzed by the cold, sickened by the invasion of these vulgar people in his four thousand acres of parkland, what his children called The Secret Place.

And now Ena challenged this woman who just got through offering her husband one of Monette's fingers to catch fish with. Ena, he realized with a mixture of pride and fear, Ena was as solemn and formidable as Bev when she got off the school bus.

Is my mother happy or mad?

It was too dangerous. Everything wound up too tight. Gage wouldn't take the risk. He had to get them all out of there.

"Ena," he said quietly out of the side of his mouth, "shut up."

"No," Ena blazed back. "I hate her. I hope she dies."

The pregnant woman snickered again. "Who do you think you are, lady," she asked, "telling people you hope they die?"

"Who do you think you are," said Ena, "talking about using a little kid's fingers for bait?"

"That's just a joke," said the man who had been sulking and watching the whole development. "And that ain't none of your business, lady."

Monette, joined by Clifford, stared at Ena. "You shut up," Monette said. She balled her fists now at Ena. And Clifford did the same. "Shut up."

"See?" jeered the pregnant woman. "It's just a joke. And it ain't none of your business."

"Come on." Gage steered Ena and David around, never glancing back, hurrying back down the park road. Twenty feet away, he turned, whistled for the dog. The pregnant woman was standing and stretching both arms over her head, the man casting hook after hook into the glittering water. The two children chased each other.

How did he let this ugly thing happen? These four people behaving almost as caricatures of Gage's own family. He hated them. Ena was right.

I hope you die.

Back inside their own warm safe house, Ena sat again in the wing chair, curling a strand of her hair over a finger. She studied it a moment, pink as a curled-up shrimp.

"What if they really meant it, Gage?" she asked, pulling her finger free. "What if they really used one of that kid's fingers?"

She mimicked the pregnant woman, rounding her green eyes like hard green buttons, tightening her mouth. "Use one of Monette's fingers."

Gage gazed at Ena's curling finger and considered everything he had to lose in his answer. The brisk sky over four thousand acres of North Carolina parkland. David, setting up the plastic soldiers on the floor again, warm and healthy and unafraid. Bev, struggling with backward 3's at school, all her fingers intact. Bev, returning home in a few hours to ask, "Is my mother happy or mad?"

Ena, the source of their happiness or their grief, sat winding the hair over her finger again, waiting for his answer.

Ena, he understood, like the pregnant woman at The Secret Place, could kill or let live. Women like that loved and killed each other in their own way. And then closed ranks. Made you feel it was your fault.

That's a joke, lady. And it ain't none of your business.

Gage smiled. "They didn't mean it, sweetheart."

She studied him a minute. Then, "I hope you're right, Gage," she shrugged him off and closed her eyes.

Just that, and nothing he could do about it.

A.D.

When Mrs. Redwine went to the hospital to have Anthony Duke Redwine, she told the prep nurses not to shave off her pubic hair.

"Mr. Redwine said that was too pretty to shave off!" she shrieked up as they struggled with her fat arms and searched for a place to sink the needle.

Mrs. Redwine did something crazy each time she had a baby in the Stanly County Memorial Hospital. The prep nurses had to cut a Spencer corset off her before Alison Denise, the middle child, could get born, Mrs. Redwine insisting all the time she needed that Spencer corset for support. And the snipping and pulling of laces and steel wires, the stretching of elastic and the outright ripping to pieces of satin linings went on at mad rush to get the big fat woman free before the baby crowned right there and entered life with a flat skull.

And all the time Amber Day Redwine, the oldest, struggled toward the way out, Mrs. Redwine sat behind the door to her hospital room, protesting to everyone she had a little bitty stomachache and why didn't they leave her the hell alone?

Mr. Redwine was never around for these nativities. He brought her to the Stanly County Memorial Hospital, turned her over and then went straight back to the Olympia Cafe in Badin where he remained throughout her delivery and recovery.

Mr. Redwine wasn't big and fat like his wife, just big, well over six feet tall, and talked like a wind-up toy. The word pipsqueak applied to Mr. Redwine's voice. Not his size.

Nothing about Mr. and Mrs. Redwine, in fact, applied to the three kids they had. Amber Day, Alison Denise, and Anthony

Duke Redwine were the three best-looking kids ever seen in Badin. Blond, with wide dark eyes and perpetually rosy faces, these three stopped total strangers on the street.

"What a beautiful child!" the strangers complimented Mrs. Redwine rolling Amber Day in her carriage.

They bent over, took the little girl's hand in theirs, smiled, melted. "Oh, what a beautiful child!" they complimented again, then looked up at Mrs. Redwine and couldn't help adding, "I guess she looks like her daddy."

And when Alison Denise was born, Badin said, "Well, we just hope she's as pretty as her big sister."

She was prettier. There would be Mrs. Redwine, big as a ship under sail, rolling the new baby down the street, pulling Amber Day by a hand, accepting compliments all around.

"How did you do it, Betty Lou!" exclaimed her friends. "They're dolls! Just dolls!"

Anthony Duke, the last and the only boy, was the prettiest of them all. Mrs. Redwine let his blond hair grow long and curly until he was two years old. Then she announced, "Well, I'm getting his hair cut off. I'm damned sick of people saying 'Oh, what a pretty little girl! Oh, what three pretty little girls, Betty Lou!' So he gets his hair whacked off today in the barbershop. It's time he knew what he was."

Off she sailed to the Quality Barbershop and stood there while the barber whacked off Anthony Duke's blond hair and Anthony Duke screamed and Amber Day and Alison Denise stood there laughing at him and he screamed more. This done, Mrs. Redwine was back out the door and down the street, jerking her three beauties behind, Anthony Duke sucking a lollipop fuzzed in blond hairs.

"That's done," she said, "and I did it."

Mrs. Redwine was given to abrupt final decisions. Stubborn. Theatrical. And the fact remained in Badin, short hair or long, Badin never saw three better-looking kids than Anthony Duke, Alison Denise, and Amber Day Redwine.

All Mrs. Redwine's kids had the initials A and D. After the death, *Anno domini.* In the year of the Lord. To a more mythical or literary woman, these letters might have symbolized something: time or old age or fate or God. But Mrs. Redwine got all their names off television. Day after day, waiting for each of her three kids to ripen within her, she had sat looking at television, taking keen notice of the names of soap opera heroes, game contestants, and the stars of the Mystery Movie. Once she hit on Amber Day's name, she stuck to the two initials, A and D.

"My daddy named me Betty Lou," she scoffed to her friends. "Betty Lou! A *common* name. And I'll tell you one thing."

She glanced around dramatically, pulling her friends closer to hear this one thing she'd tell them.

"I'll tell you my kids might not have anything else in the world, but they're going to have a decent name. A pretty name. Something unusual."

"I don't like unusual names," said one of her friends, a nervous short woman christened Leola Laughinghouse.

"Then, Leola, you ought to be named Betty Lou," declared Mrs. Redwine.

Abrupt, stubborn, theatrical, she didn't deal in symbolic names. But she made sure everything lived up to its name. Whether she was insisting her pubic hair be left untouched or that her Spencer corset remain on her big fat laboring body or if she plainly lied to the entire obstetrical staff of the Stanly County Memorial Hospital that she wasn't pregnant, just had a little bitty stomachache, Mrs. Betty Lou Redwine viewed the world on her terms. Nobody else's.

The three kids seemed unaware of all this. They reached high school in the late 1960s unblemished. They had no excess body fat. No pipsqueak voices. Badin couldn't get over the miracle of it: these three good-looking creations had come out of such awful stuff like Mr. and Mrs. Redwine.

Then Mr. Redwine found something prettier than Mrs. Redwine's pubic hair, something more unusual than his kids' television names. He found another woman in Badin and ran off with her to West Palm Beach. This happened at Christmas.

Now the world was viewed on somebody else's abrupt and stubborn and theatrical terms. Towering above them, his squeaky voice aggravating the chilly air, Mr. Redwine told Amber Day and Alison Denise and Anthony Duke before he left Badin:

"I'll keep in touch with you. I'll send you money every year on your birthday. I'll send you as many dollars as you are old. *Every* year."

To Mrs. Redwine, Mr. Redwine didn't say a whole lot. "Betty Lou, I'm getting the hell out of here."

"What am I supposed to do?" she demanded, insisting still on her terms.

"There's nothing you can do." He blasted her terms.

"What about these three fine children?"

"They're still three fine children."

He left.

And after lumbering up and down the apartment, hollering and cursing through teeth and tears, Mrs. Redwine collapsed in bed, a quivering pile of insult and injury.

"I'm never getting up out of this bed again!" she declared to her kids. "Never!"

"It's Christmas," said Alison Denise.

"We haven't got the Christmas tree yet," said Anthony Duke.

"Mama, you're so stupid," said Amber Day.

"I can't help it. I'm never getting up out of this bed *again!*"

The three went downstairs and sat around the cold blear-eyed television. Dust circled the lamps and ashtrays. A bunch of Christmas cards straggled across the coffee table.

"This.pisses me off," said Anthony Duke.

"Pisses me off, too," agreed Alison Denise. "It's Christmas."

"So, it's Christmas, and everybody's pissed off. Now what?" threw in Amber Day. "Daddy ran off with another woman. Mama's decided to go to bed and be a martyr. Now what?"

"We don't have a Christmas tree." Anthony Duke pointed to the living-room window. "I bet everybody on this whole damned street has got a Christmas tree, but us."

"You think that's something? You think that's a problem?" Amber Day glared. "Listen up:

"Today John David Stupid Ass Matlock told me we were getting too serious. He wants to go out with other people. He's not taking me to the Christmas dance this year. And Mama thinks she got the shaft! I'd like to tell her about getting the shaft."

"I know who he's taking." Alison Denise rolled her eyes.

"Who?"

"Dana Vann."

"Dana Vann! Dana Vann doesn't even have any boobs! Besides that, she goes with Dean Poole."

"I don't care. Dean Poole's in Korea. J.D.'s taking Dana Vann. You'll see."

Alison Denise pulled up her jeans and inspected the stubble on her bare legs. "Yep, old Dana No-Boobs Vann."

"What's that got to do with anything?" cut in Anthony Duke. "We still don't have a Christmas tree."

"How do you know who he's taking?" Amber Day slid onto the sofa beside Alison Denise and took hold, lightly, although threateningly, of her V-neck sweater.

"It doesn't matter how I know. I know," returned Alison Denise. "Don't you stretch my V-neck sweater."

"Oh, shit fire," said Amber Day. "Shit fire! Some Christmas this is. John David J.D. Stupid Ass Matlock and Dana No-Boobs Vann. Jesus Christ. My daddy gone to West Palm Beach, my mama gone to bed to get even, and now my boyfriend dumps me for a girl with absolutely no boobs! What else?"

"No Christmas tree," added Anthony Duke.

"If you say Christmas tree one more time, I'll kill you," threatened Amber Day Redwine.

"Christmas tree," sneered Anthony Duke.

This went on several days, Amber Day and Anthony Duke Redwine outdoing themselves in maledictions, Alison Denise Redwine holding a middle ground, and Mrs. Betty Lou Redwine recumbent, her bed of affliction sagging and wheezing as she turned from side to side, pounding each word like a nail:

"I'm never going to get up out of this bed *again!*"

"Don't pay any attention," said Amber Day, "she'll get up."

Asked Alison Denise: "When?"

"I don't know. She just will."

"I don't care if she ever gets up again or not," said Anthony Duke. "All I care about is getting up a Christmas tree."

"You'll get one," promised Amber Day.

"When?"

"I don't know. You just will, that's all."

On Christmas Eve, Mr. Redwine called his three kids long distance from West Palm Beach. "Hey, how're you all?" he squeaked through the wire.

Answered Amber Day: "We're fine, Daddy. How're you? What's it like in West Palm Beach?"

"Is this Amber Day?"

"Yes, Daddy."

"I'm fine, honey. Fine. How's Alison Denise?"

"She's fine, too, Daddy."

"How's Anthony Duke?"

"He's fine. Daddy, we're all fine. What's it like there, Daddy?" Amber Day, beginning to weary of his conversation, listened to her mother sigh and flop over upstairs. Flop, whoosh, *Oh, god!*

A small silence between them. "How's your mother?"

"She's in bed."

"Is she sick?"

"No, she's just in bed."

"Hey, tell him we don't have a Christmas tree," hissed Anthony Duke across the room. "Tell him we're never going to get a god-damned Christmas tree and it's his fault!"

"Tell him J.D.'s taking a girl with no boobs to the dance tonight in your place and it's his fault, too!" giggled Alison Denise.

Squeaked Mr. Redwine: "Listen, honey, I got to go. You all be good and take care of your sick mother and have a merry Christmas. And remember, honey," he halted.

"Remember what?" said Amber Day. She couldn't help the irritation in her voice.

"Remember, I'm going to send you money on your birthday every year. As many dollars as you are old! You tell everybody, Amber Day."

"Daddy," suggested Amber Day, a hand on her hip, "why don't you just go to hell?"

But he'd hung up. The wire crackled in her ear.

"Well?" asked the others, "what'd you find out?"

"I found out everybody's fine." She jammed the phone back on the wall. "Just fine."

"That's a bunch of bull," concluded Anthony Duke. "Didn't he even say anything about West Palm Beach?"

Upstairs the floor shuddered as Mrs. Redwine flopped again.

That Christmas Eve many things happened that were abrupt and stubborn and downright theatrical. Amber Day went into the Badin dime store and bought a small artificial Christmas tree. It had been a cedar, bristly and fragrant. Now it stood three feet from a wooden X, all its foliage crusted by white spray paint, stiff as a board.

"He won't like it," warned Alison Denise, watching her sister carry the white tree down the street.

"He won't have to," said Amber Day.

They set it on the coffee table and draped a string of lights around its white stubble. Alison Denise examined the other ornaments.

"You want to put any of this junk on it, too?"

"No, this is enough."

"He's not going to like it," Alison Denise reminded.

"I don't care, dammit. It's a Christmas tree." Amber Day plugged in the one string of lights and the little cedar winked red, green, yellow.

"There," gestured Amber Day, "a damned Christmas tree."

"That's not a damned Christmas tree," jeered Anthony Duke when he saw what they had done.

"It's her fault," said Alison Denise. "I told her you wouldn't like it."

"I knew it was her fault before I ever got here and saw it," said Anthony Duke. "That's *not* a Christmas tree."

"It's all the Christmas tree you get, smart ass, so shut up," said Amber Day.

"The shit you say." Anthony Duke thumped one of the little branches. White cedar flaked over the coffee table.

"The shit *you* say," Amber Day threatened. "Anything else and this Christmas tree goes up your ass."

"You'd look funny walking around Badin with a Christmas tree stuck up your ass," said Alison Denise. She flopped across the sofa and put her feet on the coffee table, smearing the white flakes.

"Actually," admitted Alison Denise, "I think it's sort of cute." Red, green, and yellow lights winked over her face.

"The shit you *both* say," scoffed Anthony Duke. "Any presents I get are not going under that."

"Any presents you get can go up your ass with the tree," said Amber Day.

Said Alison Denise: "Why don't you all just shut the hell up? It's Christmas."

They got supper ready. Alison Denise was arranging a tray for Mrs. Redwine when Amber Day said, "I know how to get Mama out of that bed."

She got a big bottle of milk of magnesia and stirred every drop into her mother's food, into the creamed potatoes, into the gravy, into the blue cheese salad dressing.

"She'll never notice it," said Amber Day.

Alison Denise watched with amazed glee.

"Just to make sure, though." Amber Day glanced around the kitchen. She took a package of Ex-Lax and crumbled up the doses into Mrs. Redwine's chocolate pie, poking little holes through the filling and smoothing them over with a knife. She sprinkled Ex-Lax across the meringue like chocolate garnish.

"She'll never know what hit her."

"What're you trying to do, kill Mama?" Alison Denise touched one finger to the Ex-Lax on the meringue.

"Yes," admitted Amber Day.

When supper was done, the dishes stacked in the kitchen, when Mrs. Redwine had flopped once again in her martyr's bed, settled for a Christmas Eve of grief and accusation, Amber Day got ready for the dance.

"I wouldn't go to a dance by myself," said Alison Denise.

"I'm not going by myself. You all are going with me." Amber Day shook out her party skirt and fastened a red velvet bandeau in her blond hair. "Both of you."

"I'm not going to that dance. I'm not invited."

"Nobody's invited. It's a school dance, you know that. Go tell Anthony Duke to get ready."

"He won't go."

"Tell him."

"I hate you," said Alison Denise Redwine.

"I don't care what you hate," said Amber Day.

Despite their loud protestations, their curiosity got the better of Alison Denise and Anthony Duke and they accompanied Amber Day through a frosty glittering night to the Badin High School gymnasium, Anthony Duke swearing every step:

"I'm not going to this damned dance with you, Amber Day. You can't make me. And I'm not dancing a single dance with you when I get there, either, dammit."

"You don't have to," she promised. "You don't have to do anything you don't want to. That's a fact of life."

At the punch table, as Alison Denise smirked, Amber Day said "Hello" to John David Matlock. She took a cup and turned to Dana Vann who stared at both her and Alison Denise with big startled blue eyes. Amber Day started to say, "Hello, No Boobs" to Dana, then thought better of it, just smiled.

"What're you doing here?" demanded J.D.

"I can come to a dance, if I want to." Amber Day put the punch cup on the table.

"My little brother's looking for you," she said to Dana. "He's been telling me and Alison Denise all day how you're the best-looking thing walking in the eighth grade. Didn't he, Alison Denise?"

Alison Denise looked across the gym to where Anthony Duke was knocking around the floor, elbowing his friends, stepping on girls' feet. "I can't stand this," she said and moved off toward her own friends.

Amber Day took hold of John David's jacket and pulled him on the dance floor. As they glided around the gym under big red and green festoons and the basketball nets shimmering with tinsel, she smiled:

"Don't think I'm going to forget this. Don't think I'm going to let this go by for free, John David Matlock. And don't think for one shit-fire minute that I'm getting serious about you."

Amber Day twirled under his arm, her party skirt sibilant, her velvet bandeau lush, her blond hair delicate and inviolable.

"Don't think I could ever get serious about somebody who'd dump me for a girl with absolutely no boobs to her name."

She left him on the dance floor, returning to the punch table where Dana Vann still stood, staring with bigger eyes. "What's the matter with you?" Amber Day asked.

"Nothing," managed Dana.

"Then have some punch." Amber Day ladled a slopping splash of cranberryginger ale down the front of Dana's dress.

The punch spread through every thread of Dana Vann's white taffeta front and showed every little wire circled around in her Sweetheart Shapely Training Bra. The Sweetheart Shapely Training Bra kept its dimensions, pushing blindly through fiber-fillings despite the thick red splotch.

Amber Day Redwine gazed at Dana Vann's dress. She suggested in a wise concerned old-woman tone, "You better put cold water on that when you get home."

The three Redwines walked home in a frostier, more glittering dark, Anthony Duke's pockets stuffed with cookies and mints, Alison Denise flourishing a cigarette a friend had given her.

"You think I ought to smoke this cigarette?" she asked Amber Day.

"Whatever."

"I'd smoke it," said Anthony Duke.

"This is a Salem, cork filter," bragged Alison Denise. She rolled the cigarette between cold fingers. "I'm going to smoke it right now."

She put it to her lips.

"You don't even have a match," said Amber Day.

Christmas morning. As little kids through Badin raced to their trees to see what Santa Claus left them, the three Redwine kids woke to thunder as Mrs. Redwine raced from her bed to the bathroom.

"I told you," said Amber Day from her side of the room.

"I hate and despise you," said Alison Denise, pulling the cover over her head.

Through the wall they heard Anthony Duke exclaim, "Jesus! She's going to stomp the whole house down!"

And stomp it down, she did, all Christmas morning. Keeping a clear track between her bed and the bathroom, Mrs. Redwine sprang up with an agility amazing to her three kids who gathered in the living room around the white cedar.

She lumbered across the floor over their heads as they opened their presents and grimaced at each sag of the bed, each resounding shudder of the plumbing.

They tried, though, to ignore her.

"I know every one of these come from Daddy," said Anthony Duke, examining the tags on his presents. "But how come Santa Claus writes just like you?"

"Because I'm Santa Claus," said Amber Day.

Said Alison Denise: "Nobody in this family believes in Santa Claus," the Salem cigarette, unlit, in her mouth.

Amber Day watched the Salem bobble as her sister spoke. "I do," she said.

"The shit you say," sneered Anthony Duke. "I'll show you Santa Claus. Just you watch this."

And he picked up the little white tree, jerking the lights from the plug, walked to the front door and threw it in a wide clattering arc to Spruce Street.

"Hey," he yelled at the little kids on their new bikes, the little kids pushing Tiny Tears and Chatty Cathy in new doll carriages. "Hey! See what Santa Claus brought!"

He returned to the coffee table, collected all his presents and threw them one by one into Spruce Street after the tree.

"Anthony Duke has finally gone crazy," observed Alison Denise, taking the Salem from her mouth and tucking it up her sleeve. She scooped her presents off the coffee table.

Anthony Duke came back. "And if I thought I could, goddammit, I'd throw you in the street, too, Amber Day. You're so smart. You're so damned spoiled and stuck up, all the time thinking you can fix it, you can make it okay. For two cents, I'd throw you in the street."

Amber Day gazed at him. She dug into her jeans, brought out two cents and put them on the coffee table.

"Go ahead," she said, "throw me."

"And Amber Day has finally gone crazy," declared Alison Denise. "I'm stuck in a house full of crazy people for Christmas."

The stairs creaked and their mother appeared in the living-room door. She tottered a moment, her fuzzy robe billowing, then she put a hand to the wall to steady herself as she demanded, "What're you all doing?"

"It's Christmas, Mama," said Alison Denise.

"And we don't have a Christmas tree," said Anthony Duke.

"I guess you all think that's my fault," said Mrs. Redwine, wrapping her robe around her and tying the sash with a self-righteous flair.

"I guess you all think I don't have enough on my mind with your sorry daddy running off to West Palm Beach with that woman, and then me waking up with this virus, you all think I've still got to celebrate Christmas and get you a Christmas tree?"

She clasped a hand to her gut. "Your sorry daddy's going to pay for this. He's going to pay for every minute of my misery."

Mrs. Redwine thundered back upstairs to the bathroom, affirming, "He's going to pay!"

Yes, thought Amber Day, he's going to send us money every year on our birthday, he's going to send as many dollars as we are old.

Up and down Spruce Street, all through Badin, North Carolina, lights winked on perfect Christmas trees, red, green, yellow. Bells jingled. Kids laughed. People kissed each other. It was Christmas. *Anno domini.*

"This is a bitch of a Christmas," said Alison Denise. She pulled the Salem out of her sleeve. It was broken in two. Little bits of menthol-tainted tobacco sprinkled through her fingers.

"You said it," agreed Anthony Duke, glaring at Amber Day, "and it's her fault."

"Well," said Amber Day mildly, getting up and walking to the windows. She looked at the little kids on bikes circling the white dime-store tree in the middle of the street. Two little girls collected Anthony Duke's jettisoned presents, sneaking glances back at the apartment.

"Well," she affirmed more confidently and smiled, while overhead plumbing gurgled and her big fat mother thundered back and forth, alive and healthy as sunshine, definitely up and out of the bed.

"What do you know about anything?"

BILLY GOAT

Paint dabs across the rough canvas, fleshing out Kate Poole's arms, her dark eyes that flash and dart, her short hair cut in dark bangs thick to the brow, and her grasping, claiming little hands. Seven years old, she does not want to pose like this, like some kind of a baby.

"Preston!" prompts her mother Zandra, the painter, "make her be still."

And Uncle Preston, her daddy's younger brother with whom they share the house, takes charge of Kate, holds her on his lap and tells ugly little stories to calm her down while her mother paints the portrait.

Outside their pale yellow-boarded house, North Carolina sweeps off into thin blue distances. Old women who have lived into the 1990s, tough old women nobody wants to take care of, root up potatoes in flat gardens edged by plum thickets while the aluminum smelter in the middle of town pours out long, malleable, silver-white ingots breathing flame. They become part of the ugly little stories.

"Once a big old billy goat belonged to a farmer and his wife and little girl," begins Uncle Preston over Kate's busy head. She bumps her head against his gray sweats, rolls her eyes back to look.

"Kate!"

She returns her gaze to the front, still listening to the story.

"This billy goat was bad news. He played tricks and cut up all over the place and took advantage, and the farmer said he would punish him if he didn't quit it."

Light blooms in the open windows of the studio, which is just a big upstairs bedroom from which they can see the towers of the aluminum smelter. The sour smell of paint loads the air and Kate's mother smiles, dabbing at the rosy skin beneath the brush.

Uncle Preston shifts, kisses the back of Kate's dark head. Already she is mellowing under his syllables, eyes wide-fixed, listening and waiting.

"It didn't make any difference to the old billy goat what anybody said. He kept on doing things, kicking over the milk cans, butting stuff off the table, scattering the chickens in the yard. 'I have warned you and warned you, goat,' said the farmer. 'Now you have to pay for this.' And while his wife and his little girl held the billy goat down, the farmer started to skin him alive with a big sharp knife."

Her arms and the back of her neck prickle at this and Kate shivers. "That's a lie," she says. "I don't believe it."

Uncle Preston kisses her head again. "You don't have to," he affirms and picks up the story.

"But the billy goat was too smart. He got away from the farmer's wife and his little girl and started running, half-skinned, down the road from the farmer. And he ran away to the woods and stayed there. The woods right outside." He nods toward the window. Kate stretches her eyes toward the window, too.

"Preston," says her mother, "turn her a little to the left."

"Did it bleed?" demands Kate Poole as she is being turned a little to the left.

"You bet," replies Uncle Preston.

"Did it hurt?"

"Like the *devil.*"

"How did he get well?"

"Listen," says Uncle Preston, "the farmer and his wife and his little girl got along okay and nothing bad happened. Then after a whole year, one night the billy goat came up and knocked on the front door. When the farmer opened up, he was shocked to see that old goat, still half-skinned, still alive. No hair growing on the skinned part, though. It was just kind of bald and like a scar."

Kate blinks, smells the comforting stink of Uncle Preston's gray sweats, warm and rich. "Oh," she says, again, "oh," feeling her arms and neck prickle more.

"Listen, 'I am your old half-skinned billy goat,' the goat said to the farmer." Then Uncle Preston jogs out a little rhyme:

> *My horns are sharp, my hooves are bright.*
> *Give me what I want tonight,*
> *Or I'll cut your throat,*
> *For I am the old half-skinned billy goat!*

Kate sits like a stone, imagining the horror of opening the front door and finding a half-skinned billy goat. The shock of having this old goat say a little rhyme to her, jog it out at her that way. Like Uncle Preston.

"What happened then?"

"You should ask 'What did he want?'" chides Uncle Preston.

"What did he want?"

"He said, '*Give me butter and milk. Give me satin and silk.*'

'I don't have satin and silk,' said the farmer, scared to death.

'Well, then:'" Uncle Preston jogs again:

> *Give me what you have tonight,*
> *Or I'll carry you away out of Christian sight!*

"What did he give him?" asks Kate. Her fingers twist a fold of the gray sweats. She wants to make sure Uncle Preston stays there. She's half mad at him for starting this.

Kate's mother's brush spreads curiosity, wonder, excitement, a tinge of horror across the canvas. She listens to her brother-in-law's story with the same attention as the little girl. It enhances her stroke, sharpens her eye.

"Well," says Uncle Preston, shifting a leg, "he gave him all the butter and milk out of the refrigerator and then the billy goat went off. But the very next night he came right back and knocked on the front door. And the billy goat said all over again:

I am your old half-skinned billy goat.
My horns are sharp, my hooves are bright.
Give me what I want tonight,
Or I'll cut your throat,
For I am the old half-skinned billy goat!

"What did he give him then? More butter and milk?" Kate pinches up folds of her skirt along with the gray sweats. Her legs itch and she wants to get down, run outside and look at the real goats in the yard behind the house. She wants to look very hard at all of them.

"No." Uncle Preston smiles. "This time the goat said:

Give me strawberry jam and a roll,
Give me silver and a bag of gold.

'I don't have silver and a bag of gold,' said the farmer.

Well, then give me what you have tonight,
Or I'll carry you away out of Christian sight!"

"Preston," asks his sister-in-law, "where did you hear this ugly little story?" She puts down her brush and waits. Light coming from the windows behind throws a bright crown around her head and she looks like a holy picture to Kate. One of those things on the front of the Sunday School books.

"Where did you hear it?"

Uncle Preston shifts Kate on his knees. "From Michael. He made it up. I think to make me shut up when Mama made us take a nap. He always wanted me to shut up and go to sleep so he could sneak out. It's Michael's ugly little story."

"I can't believe Michael Poole made up anything."

"What happened next?" insists Kate.

"I don't know." Uncle Preston shrugs. "I always went to sleep before the end. Michael knows what happened next. Didn't he ever tell it to you, Zandra?"

"I told you, I never heard it before, Preston." She turns away and snaps shut her paints.

So, thinks Kate Poole, it's a lie. Nothing happens in that old story. No old half-skinned billy goat is coming back again to get nobody, no farmer, no farmer's wife, no little girls. It's a lie. She can't help it, though, that she shivers again on Uncle Preston's lap and demands, "Tell me the end anyhow. I want to hear the end."

"That's enough for today." Her mother moves around taking charge of things. "The light's moved already. Preston, you've sat there with her long enough. We'll work some more tomorrow."

Set free, Kate runs to the backyard to look at the little goats fenced there. She looks hard at their hooves, their curved horns, and their slanted yellow eyes. Small and playful, they follow one another jumping and butting. One of them stands on an old walnut stump and the others try to crowd him off, baaing all the time.

Kate plucks the wire fence and threatens, "Give me what I want tonight, or I'll carry you away out of Christian sight!" The little goats blink at her, baa, chew their cuds. Stupid goats, she thinks.

Two white-brown does stare. One curious little dark buck trots over to butt at Kate's hand. She studies his head, thinking he ought to be painted in her mother's portrait, not her.

Give me what I want tonight!

She picks up a rock and throws. The little goats scatter.

The pale yellow clapboard house stands in the countryside about two miles from a small North Carolina aluminum-smelting town. They inherited it together, Michael and Preston, from their mother Dana Poole, and neither will leave. The house, with goats and chickens fenced in the backyard, has green shutters pulled against the noon heat and upstairs Zandra and Kate are lying down on cool bare sheets. Uncle Preston has gone out to interview for a job, he said, at the aluminum smelter. Kate slips closer across the sheets toward her mother who sprawls, open-legged, a wet towel on her head, eyes closed. Kate's daddy Michael Poole, an exterminator, drives around with a big black spider stuck to the side of his truck. He makes good money and stays gone so much, she can barely recall the look of him, the tone of his voice echoing in the house. He is gone now and will be gone for days.

"Mother?" she puts out a hand to trace the lace insertion of Zandra's camisole, "Mother, why do we have all those goats out in the backyard?"

"For milk, you know that. Because Daddy's allergic and he has to drink it." Her mother moves away from the child's hand. "You know that."

"Daddy's not never here to drink it." Kate puts her hand back on the lace. She brightens, "Do we have them for butter?" Kate sits up, delighted with this new possibility. "Do we have them for goat butter?"

"Don't be so silly. People don't eat goat butter. What a stupid thing. Daddy's just allergic, that's all." Zandra turns completely over, away from Kate's hands and her new delight, leaving her utterly alone and unrequited.

Kate drops back down, turns the strange word *allergic* over and over her tongue, *allergic*. It sticks to the roof of her mouth, right behind her front teeth, *allergic*.

In the night, after Uncle Preston has returned and everyone gone to bed for good, the heat slacked off a little, Kate Poole wakes, hears whispering, her mother's laugh low and throaty, then her uncle's responding laugh.

"Mother? Uncle Preston?" She waits in the dark.

Nothing.

No movement outside her door. Only the faintest ba-baaing from the goats in the yard. She imagines their little yellow eyes, the little beards under their chins.

Or I'll carry you away out of Christian sight.

Stupid! Kate slips from her bed and pads down the hall to her mother's room. She barely opens it and sees in the soft darkness Uncle Preston lifting himself over Zandra, then thrusting down, Zandra sighing.

"What're you doing? Kate pushes wide the door. "You stop!" Uncle Preston does stop. Both he and Zandra crane toward Kate in the door.

"It's just Kate," whispers Zandra.

"What're you doing?" Kate demands again. "I see you!"

Uncle Preston laughs, pushes away from Zandra, pulls the sheet over him. "Come here," he invites, holding out an arm. "Get in."

Kate hesitates a moment, sliding her bare feet on the slick polished floor. She doesn't entirely trust Uncle Preston. Then she brightens, "Tell me the billy goat."

"Why not?" he agrees, and she settles between her mother and Uncle Preston. "But I don't know the end," he reminds her.

"Michael does," she reminds him back. "You said."

At the mention of Kate's daddy's name, both Uncle Preston and her mother squirm. Uncle Preston hugs Kate closer. "Listen," he says, "this is a game we're playing, me and you and Zandra. And we're playing it against Michael. It's a secret game, you understand?"

He hugs Kate again. "You want to keep playing the secret game?"

She nods, flexes her toes under the sheet, drinking in the smell of Uncle Preston and her mother and herself. Nothing, she thinks, can be as good as this. Uncle Preston keeps talking about the secret game against Michael Poole and what the rules are, but Kate isn't paying attention. She drifts, snores.

For breakfast Kate Poole likes eggs beaten with sugar until her glass is full of foamy yellow sweetness. She doesn't care that the egg is still raw when she eats it, her lip a yellow smudge. She loves it and smacks and declares, "I love this to *death!* Make another one."

"That's raw, you know." Uncle Preston teases. "You're eating a *raw* egg."

Her mother observes. "Sugar helps to cook egg. It's not really raw. Something happens when you mix up the egg with the sugar. It cooks it, sort of."

"Listen to the chemistry major," scoffs Uncle Preston. "Dr. Zandra and her Nobel Prize." He breaks more eggs into the glass, spoons great mounds of sugar in with them, and beats everything with a fork until it is all goldish air and sweet delight.

"We're spoiling her," he says, watching Kate eat.

"*You're* spoiling her," corrects Zandra.

"Somebody has to," he says, wiping off his hands. "And," he adds with a wise air, "it's good for her."

"Ha," scoffs Zandra. "It's not good for her. It's good for the chickens. Gives them something to do. Lay more eggs." She puts down her coffee cup. "Gives *you* something to do."

"And what, darling Zandra," Preston asks, smiling across the table, "does it give you to do?"

"I've got plenty to do." She smiles back at him, her lips very full and firm.

"Does Michael believe that?"

"It doesn't matter what Michael believes." Kate's mother shakes a cigarette from the pack on the table between them, lights it, continues smiling.

Michael Poole, the exterminator with the truck, knows the end of the billy-goat story, Kate remembers. Her own big bald-headed daddy. And, she sits wondering, maybe when he comes back, he'll bring the end of the story with him. After all, Uncle Preston already said he made it up in the first place just to make him, Uncle Preston, shut up and go to sleep. Right here in this house which they both own.

Kate snuffles the last of the sugary egg, well pleased. She'll ask Michael the first thing, What happened to the old half-skinned billy goat?

But when Michael Poole finally gets there, he's not in a mood to tell stories. He roars into the drive, his truck throwing gravel, the big black spider hanging like some ugly abnormality from its door. Upstairs in the studio, Kate twists around from her pose and watches him walk toward the house. He pauses, lights a cigarette, then shoves the door.

"Zandra?"

Kate's mother ignores this. "Turn back around," she commands Kate. "Do I have to go get Uncle Preston to hold you still again?"

Kate doesn't turn. "Yes," she says, "go get Uncle Preston." She blinks against the light, listens to Michael's truck popping in the heat, follows his tread up the stairs. "Go get Uncle Preston to hold me still."

"Turn around!" Her mother raps a brush against the easel like a schoolteacher calling for attention.

"Zandra, didn't you hear me?" Michael is in the studio and the stink of his cigarette floats with the smell of the paint. "I called you soon as I came in the front door."

Zandra dips her brush in dark paint, loads it, applies the dark to Kate's bangs. "I heard you. Everybody heard you, Michael. So?"

"So, I might like an answer. Something easy, like 'Oh, hello, Michael. I'm glad to see you, Michael. I love you, Michael.'"

With each example, Kate's daddy gets closer to Zandra, standing finally behind her. He flicks ash in the dark paint, then stubs his cigarette there.

Zandra looks at the cigarette. Smoke still wisping up from it stings her eyes. "Hello, Michael," she says. "I'm glad to see you, Michael. I love you, Michael."

Kate has turned now to sit and stare at both her parents. She is as good a model as Zandra could wish right then. Nothing moves. Her hands are clasped in the way Zandra wants, her face set, her dress spread, her ankles crossed, her bare feet. Kate is the best portrait anybody could ever paint right then. Still life. She is figuring out what kind of people she came from.

Michael Poole gazes awhile at Zandra. Then he shrugs and leaves. Kate and Zandra listen to his steps down the stairs. Zandra says, "Fuck you, Michael," and crossing to the big mirror she keeps on the wall of the studio, studies her face. She picks the cigarette from the dark paint and uses it to paint one streak across each cheek, another down her nose and chin.

"Mother!" exclaims Kate, wriggling off her pose, "what you doing that for? You look like an Indian!"

Zandra thinks awhile. "I am an Indian," she says. "I'm going to scalp him."

Kate thinks of her daddy scalped. She knows what that means. She's seen enough movies on television. Her mother with a scalp hanging off her belt. Except Zandra doesn't wear belts. Except

Michael doesn't have enough hair to make a good scalp to hang off anything. Michael's hair, the same dark brown as Kate's, has slipped down behind his ears. What there is left clings thick and curled against his collar, the top of his head mottled gold and brown. He wears a dark blue Greek fisherman's cap to cover his head.

But Kate thinks about Michael Poole getting scalped anyway. Her mother would grab the dark blue cap, hack it under the brim, then with one sickening yank scalp it off her daddy's poor old bald head. Kate grins.

"Wouldn't hurt him none," she says.

"What?" Zandra is staring out the window, the paint still gleaming on her face.

"Daddy," says Kate Poole. "It wouldn't hurt him none if you scalped him."

Uncle Preston is there for dinner, laughing, passing plates, like some kind of sunny generous clown between Michael and Zandra. Kate could almost scorn him for this, except she is fascinated to see it all happening. These are my people, she calculates. Zandra and Michael and my Uncle Preston, they all hate each other to death. Then quickly amends, They all *love* each other to death, too. Loving looks, to her, to be the same as hating right then. The secret game, maybe. The game against Michael Poole that has rules. But Kate doesn't bother herself about such distinctions.

"What's the end of the billy goat?" she blurts. Michael has just lit a fresh cigarette and sits propped over his plate, chin in both hands, eyes shut against the smoke.

"What?" He blinks at her, smiles slightly. She knows Michael likes her. In spite of everything, Kate can count on Michael liking her a lot. Uncle Preston and Mother can have all the secret games against Michael they want, she thinks. In the end, he will still like me.

"That old half-skinned billy goat you told to Uncle Preston." Kate holds her fork like a conductor's baton. "What happened in the end of the story?"

Michael clears his throat, laughs, takes a deep draw. "God," he says. "I hadn't thought about that in a hundred years." Then he looks at Kate, smiles again. "Why, baby, doesn't *he* know the end?"

"Uncle Preston said you would!" Kate can't hold back the disappointment, even though she sees how much it also disappoints Michael. "Uncle Preston *said!*" Her voice sharpens.

Michael shrugs, looks at Preston. "What else did Uncle Preston say?"

"He said you made it up."

Uncle Preston passes the rolls. "Look," he offers. "Maybe that old goat ran off and never came back. Maybe he got tired of coming to the farmer's house all the time and asking for stuff. Maybe he just kept coming back and asking for stuff until finally there was nothing left in the house to give him. You think?"

"Maybe." Zandra butters a roll. "Maybe he got married and aggravated his family for the rest of his life. Maybe." She breaks off a piece and lifts it to her mouth. "Maybe he drove around in a truck and killed bugs for a living."

"That's what Daddy does." Kate Poole is at first delighted with this observation, then she knows it's not good and shuts up fast, her lips clamped with the effort.

Michael and Kate and Uncle Preston all watch Zandra chew the roll, swallow, then sip some iced tea.

"Why don't you just say it, Zandra?" sneers Michael Poole. "Quit playing games and just say it."

At this, Kate perks. "It's a secret game against *you!* We played it."

"Shut up," hisses her mother.

"What secret game?" Michael blinks, knocks the ash from his cigarette.

"Shut up!" commands Zandra. "I mean it, shut up."

"I mean it, too," says Michael. "Who played the secret game, baby?"

He coaxes and Kate is eager to give him what he wants.

"I got in the bed with them and we played it together against you."

"Michael." Uncle Preston puts a hand out, "Michael, it's not what you think. Zandra." He turns, a hand out to her. "Zandra, tell him."

"Oh, shut up, Preston." Michael's face is as venomous as the black spider on his truck. "Nobody needs to tell me anything. I can see. I can hear. I can, goddamnit, *smell*, Preston."

Michael rises, ashes the last of his cigarette. "I can smell you all over her."

"You beast. You disgusting animal." Zandra doesn't rise, doesn't even deepen her voice. She continues to butter her roll and sip her iced tea. "You can see and hear and smell whatever you want to."

Then she does rise and stares straight down the table at Michael Poole. "But so can I, goddamnit, Michael. So can *I.*"

"And what does that mean?"

"That means, Michael, that you don't come in here hollering and screaming at us and making insinuations when you yourself have been out catting around." Zandra balls a fist. "Smell? You want to talk about *smell,* Michael?"

Kate, fork still in hand, opens her mouth and bawls. It's all she knows to do when they are like this. Her face reddens and turns shiny with tears as her incontestable bawling increases.

"Now, look." Michael glares at Zandra and Uncle Preston. "It's not enough for you to carry on in my house behind my back, but you have to get my baby upset, too?"

"Your house?" Now Uncle Preston rises, sharpens his own voice. "This is not your house, Michael. This is my house, too."

"Well, then, Preston," Michael threatens, "see what you can do about getting your house in order. Because if you can't, Preston, I can."

"What does that mean?"

Michael Poole pulls on his blue cap. "That means someday I'm going to come back and you won't be here."

Uncle Preston follows him out to the truck, "Michael! Michael, *listen!*"

At the table, Kate's bawling subsides. She hiccups, snuffles in her napkin.

"Satisfied?" Zandra pours more iced tea, sits down again.

Kate nods. Michael's truck grinds off into the fading daylight. Uncle Preston comes back, the screen door slamming behind. "I can't stand this," he declares to Zandra.

"You don't have to," she says. "Just look at it the way Michael does."

"And how is that?" Uncle Preston takes his seat, watching her. Kate rolls her clammy napkin in a long bunny ear.

Zandra wipes her mouth. "Michael can't throw you out. He can't prove anything. That's the thing about Michael. He can't throw anybody out. He can't prove anything. All he can do is come back."

Kate watches Uncle Preston watching her mother and her mother watching Uncle Preston back, hard. All of them hard and intent. The long bunny ear flops open in her lap.

"He didn't know the end of the story," she accuses. "You said he knew the end of the billy goat."

Neither Zandra nor Uncle Preston look at her. They don't take their eyes off each other. And she knows, finally, there is no end to the billy goat story. It keeps going and going. Asking for things. Until you go to sleep. Stupid, stupid!

In the middle of the night Kate Poole sneaks down the hall to her mother's studio. The portrait stares at her from the easel. For a minute she hesitates, isn't sure, then shakes off the feeling. Kate squeezes paint deliberately. In the pale light of the stars, the faint shrinking moon, she can tell it is alizarin crimson, her favorite, and she's encouraged to squeeze a long, long strand of it down Zandra's palette. She takes the heaviest brush and carefully, methodically, loads alizarin crimson all over the portrait, giving herself big clown lips, a cherry nose, bloody cheeks. And raises off the top of her head, out of those glossy dark and perfect bangs, two stubby but distinctive horns growing larger with the gleeful baa-baa sneering in her throat.

TANSY

Tansy wants men in the house since C.D. died. Their voices, the rough brush-up of their clothes, and their smells. She promises me and Yolanda, squeezing our hands, C.D. is back. That makes Yolanda so mad, Yolanda's hair stands up worse than usual, and I think she's going to kill Tansy this time. Yolanda slaps off Tansy's hands, shut up, C.D. is dead and not back, shut up.

Then everything shifts into a breathless search, Tansy running around, Yolanda trying to stop her, and me following, keeping up with them.

Tansy runs to the door and calls to Mr. York stumbling across the new snow, his old navy wool peacoat brightened by the cold, Come in, don't try to sneak off.

This makes Yolanda madder. Mr. York has a leather helmet with ear flaps hanging down. And black galoshes that buckle halfway up his leg. He comes in like a kind of clumsy old dog, not knowing whether to wag his tail or do what. I was on my way to the post office, he offers, looking around.

Don't say anything, I warn Yolanda. She glares and pours coffee up to the top of Mr. York's cup. I can tell it scalds him through the thin handle of C.D. and Tansy's china cup. Yolanda got one out on purpose to burn him.

Mr. York manages a little sip, blinks as it scalds down his chin. Yolanda pulls out her turtleneck and smiles into it, her habit she thinks nobody sees. Tansy gazes at the china cup and chuckles like Yolanda is a friend the same as always, the same as me.

When Mr. York puts the cup on the mantel, Tansy rubs her face against his navy wool. I like men in the house, she whispers, C.D. died last month before it snowed.

She looks up at him, her eyes like blue water. She breathes the wool and watches him.

Shut up, Yolanda pushes Tansy away from Mr. York's old peacoat and throws the china cup to the floor. I can't help it, she glares, I can't help it.

Mr. York stands there wanting me to stop things. When C.D. died last month, I start telling him.

Tansy arranges the china pieces, No, she says, he's *here.* C.D.'s right *here.*

Yolanda pulls her turtleneck again, I hate you, Tansy, she hisses deep down to her breasts.

Mr. York gets out fast, Tansy not following, but arranging the china pieces on the rug. I'll see y'all, he says, swinging the door firmly.

I hear the snow squeak under his galoshes and it's a comforting natural sound, like Christmas and sleigh rides, just plain healthy.

C.D. smells like snow, remarks Tansy, and like coffee, too. She deposits the china pieces on the mantel.

I kneel to examine the wet splotch on the rug, a few warm drops of coffee spangle the nap, and when I lift my fingers, the coffee smell is as comforting and healthy as the sound of the snow squeaking under Mr. York's galoshes.

This is the way our life is. Tansy is the one who goes out and tries things, and it worries Yolanda who criticizes, and then I'm expected to figure it out.

Last summer Tansy swam right into C.D. hanging off the side of Morrow Mountain pool, in the ten-feet water, in the bright July noon, too bright and too hot to see good with chlorine swelling her nose and burning her eyes. She could tell C.D. hated her bathing cap. Women wearing bathing caps are the ugliest thing in the world, he told her later, after they'd dated awhile. Women wearing bathing caps and women showing their toes in shoes. I can't stand a woman to show her toes.

Don't you like my toes, Tansy said, shoving a sandal straight at him where C.D. could see her painted toenails, don't you like red toenail polish?

C.D., she reported to me and Yolanda, had grinned, bent down and lifted her foot and kissed all her painted toenails. I meant old women, he corrected himself, I didn't mean you.

Yolanda said Tansy made that up. Anyhow, Tansy could tell he hated the bathing cap, so she said something like, well, kiss my foot, C.D., and swam off. Yolanda and me were watching this, C.D. so good-looking and his shoulders big from lifting weights, C.D., we knew, was too old for Tansy. She knew it and she didn't care. Kiss my foot, C.D., she'd said. Tansy already figured she'd have C.D. looking at her some better way, some sweet loving way, even if we didn't.

She took her time climbing out of the pool, peeling off that ugly bathing cap, C.D. watching, Yolanda and me watching him watching. He was in the navy, Tansy told us in her breathless way, shaking out her dark hair, he's slept with a hundred women.

Has he got a tattoo? Yolanda sneered. Tansy said, I don't know what C.D.'s got, and all the time C.D. watching.

Then somebody fell off the board backward and splashed C.D. and he got out, disgusted, and lit a cigarette, which was against the rules, and walked over to Tansy and she took it from between his lips and just as she put it to hers and dragged, the lifeguard blew his whistle and yelled, no smoking in this pool! and we died laughing.

That night Yolanda and me sat on the porch smoking our own cigarettes and drinking up a bottle of awful chianti just so we could stick melted candles in the bottle for the kitchen. Yolanda had tried a new shampoo to get the electricity out of her hair and it wasn't working too good, already as her hair dried, it flew up in wild tufts. I hate my hair, she said. In fact, I hate everything I do around here, and she included the yard and the porch and me all in a ferocious glare.

Oh, shut up, I said, your hair's okay the way it is.

Yolanda swallowed some chianti, said, I ought to put this on my hair.

Then it'd fall out from the roots, I said, and we giggled and poured the rest of the stuff in the yard.

Ever since the third grade when we were best friends, we all had these parts to play, Tansy the glittering one, breathless, running out to try things, to examine the whole world, and Yolanda holding back, afraid, then criticizing. And me watching them both, amused, and admiring them both, too, Tansy and Yolanda both running back to me after awhile, demanding, what do you think, huh?

This night we sat on the porch waiting for Tansy to get back from her date with C.D. I don't like that guy, declared Yolanda. He's too old for her. There's no telling what he's doing to her right now.

On the contrary, I said, there's no telling what Tansy's doing to C.D. right now. I scratched at the cozy basket hugging the chianti bottle, dry and stiff. Tansy is more than a match for C.D., I said.

Tansy's crazy, said Yolanda, and she threw her cigarette toward the dark yard, the sparks fluttering into bright little wings.

C.D. moved into the tenant house with us. If Mr. York didn't like it, he didn't say, didn't raise our rent, just wandered around the yard, eyeing things, picking up sticks and limbs, jabbing at dandelions, and feeding his stand of azaleas and camellias bunched between his house and ours, crowding against the window of our biggest bedroom.

Which room C.D. and Tansy took and filled it up with C.D.'s weight-lifting stuff. He started Tansy on a body-building program. Darlin, he promised, you'll have a superior body once you get in the habit, darlin.

But don't show your toes, darlin, Yolanda reminded her, mimicking C.D., don't get in the habit, darlin, of letting your superior toes hang out.

Why don't you shut up, said Tansy, but she was laughing, and Yolanda, too. And after awhile, Yolanda was lifting weights with Tansy and after awhile, I was, C.D. directing the whole thing.

And as much as Yolanda hated to admit it, we liked it, and C.D. liked us liking it. He fit in like he'd been there all the time, crazy in love with Tansy, even softening poor old Yolanda, quieting her complaints. Sometimes I thought her hair appeared to be calmed down a little, but maybe I just wanted to think that.

They bought stuff, a microwave, a clear vinyl shower curtain with brilliant tropical fish printed all over it, and the china cups. C.D. was a dispatch clerk with the trucking company in Charlotte and he made enough. I know everything there is about trucking, he said, all the big lines, you wouldn't believe how it works so far in advance.

How? asked Tansy. She sat on the kitchen floor painting her toenails the same red they'd been in Morrow Mountain pool last summer. It was Halloween and Yolanda spread newspapers on the floor near Tansy and began carving a pumpkin for our porch.

How? she echoed Tansy, tell us, C.D., about how trucking works so far in advance.

The fresh smell of pumpkin mixed with Tansy's toenail polish, tangy, bright flavors in the kitchen, and I liked it, everything cozy and tight together, Tansy and Yolanda busy, me watching, and C.D. telling us stuff.

Well, for one thing, he started, right now they're shipping Easter orders. And when it gets to be Easter, they'll be shipping Christmas orders. They always ship six months so far in advance of the season.

I could tell C.D. liked to say that, *so far in advance,* and I liked to hear him say it, *so far in advance,* solid as a textbook or the evening news.

Tansy wiped off the brush, capped the bottle, and waved her toes dry. I knew that, she said. I knew that, too, said Yolanda. Okay, said C.D., so everybody knew that.

I didn't, I said, I never even heard of that, C.D.

Thank you, said C.D., smiling at me. Bring me some of that Easter stuff, I smiled back at him, bring me a bunch of bunny rabbits off the trucks, C.D.

It's nothing but shoes right now, he said, still smiling. Trucks and trucks of shoes. And then you know something, he hunkered close to me, laughing over the curiosities of the trucking industry, you know another time it'll be zippers. Trucks and trucks of zippers.

And then he was dying in the biggest room of the house, with Mr. York's camellias blooming against the window, those red petals blowing and coming loose and sticking to the glass as bright as Tansy's toenails. The azaleas weren't blooming yet, too early for them, the middle of February.

Tansy said, Look at the camellia bushes, C.D., and he looked where she said and we couldn't tell if he saw them or not. C.D. shut his eyes, slept. He'd been dying since that time in October when he was telling me about the trucks full of shoes and zippers so far in advance. A big tumor, C.D. hiding and hiding it all that time. Denial, Yolanda observed, it was denial, he had a denial system going.

This was after the surgeons, after the morphine drip, after the grim sessions with the oncologists, after we brought C.D. home and he wouldn't say anything much or look at things or even look at us much. It'll be a quick killer, Yolanda said, that kind always is.

And you can shut up, Tansy said, this is C.D., he lifts weights, he was in the navy, this is C.D. and he's back in the house now, so you can shut up.

She's got a denial system going, too, Yolanda whispered to me in the kitchen. We were fixing C.D. some supper on a tray, soft food, rice pudding and chicken dumplings. Tansy came in and got the tray, but C.D. wouldn't eat, just sipped a little orange juice through a straw. I hate all this, declared Yolanda and sat down and pulled at her turtleneck and breathed down on her breasts, her habit. I just hate it, hate it, hate it. Her hair stood up, fired with the old wild static, tufts like flames licking out from her head. After awhile, we followed Tansy to the bedroom.

Tansy lit a candle on the bureau, a long one red as the camellias outside tossing around in the weather, a candle people from the trucking company had sent in a Valentine bouquet to cheer C.D. up. She asked us to please come over and sit on the bed with her next to C.D. who still had his eyes shut, his big shoulders shrinking up and softening so fast you could almost see it happening each day.

I sat at the foot and Yolanda sat on the left side, next to the window with the camellia bushes, and Tansy sat on the right side, her hand on top of C.D.'s. The room smelled like Keri lotion and the burning candle.

C.D., Tansy asked, C.D., do you know what's happening to you? He opened his eyes, looked around at us. Tansy asked him again, C.D., do you know what's happening to you?

C.D. looked at Tansy then and there was no real expression on his face and his skin was smooth and perfect in the jumping candlelight. I'm not sure, he said.

Yolanda and me went back to the kitchen again and started washing up the supper dishes, thinking how the long red candle in C.D.'s Valentine bouquet would end up in our chianti bottle, the wax streaking down the sides, and how it would be sticking around on the chianti bottle in our kitchen in Mr. York's tenant house next summer, and C.D. would be dead.

It's not fair, is it, said Yolanda. No, I said, it's not, but nothing's fair. It's not fair, she repeated. And after awhile, Tansy came in the kitchen and her eyes were like blue water, not crying, C.D.'s not with us anymore, she announced in her breathless way, C.D.'s dead.

Then it was Yolanda and me calling Hartsell Funeral Home and Tansy sitting in the room with C.D. and staring at the camellias stuck on the window, and the last sight we had of C.D. was snow

starting to fall on the gray velvet pall Hartsell covered his face
with, we won't let him get snowed on, they promised Tansy, we'll
cover him up good when we go out.

And Tansy started wanting men in the house after that, their
voices, the rough brush-up of their clothes, and their smells. She
piles C.D.'s barbells in the middle of the floor, keeps his clothes
hanging in the closet beside hers. She puts on her old sandals,
toenails shining red as paint, and promises me and Yolanda, it's
C.D., and everything shifts into the old breathless search, and
Yolanda gets so mad she even cries.

A SLEEPING BEAUTY

Janice Vann thought she could sleep a century. Rudy Vann the Second was gone to the navy and she was pregnant again.

"When's the last time you saw your feet?" Everybody joked. She was sick of that stuff. She wanted to go to sleep. Stars could flare, explode, burn off to black cinders all in the time it might take her to shut her eyes, lie down in the middle of the bed with Dana, the three-year-old, and drop off.

It was Janice's birthday and Rudy wasn't around. Everybody else was getting ready to celebrate Janice's birthday and cheer her up and make her forget Rudy Vann the Second. They even got Dana on their side, making her run up to Janice, giggling and big-eyed, putting a sticky paw on her knee, "Mama! What you want for your birthday?"

Janice wished they'd shut the hell up and get out of the house.

But it was their house, her family.

She stretched out in bed, settling Dana like a spoon in front of her, and pretended the bed was a ship's hammock made out of canvas. Tight as a cocoon, like those Rudy told her were on the *West Virginia.*

"I didn't think I could sleep in one," Rudy grinned. "But I did. You get used to it, babe."

Janice rocked herself and grinned, recalling Rudy. "I wouldn't get used to it," she whispered now. "Would you, Dana?" Then chanted, "Rudy Vann. Rudy Vann. Rudy Vann."

She hummed it through her nose, rocking herself and Dana to sleep.

"Mama," drowsed Dana, "shut up and sing the boat."

71

"Lightly row, lightly row," Janice hoarsed the nursery words, "in our little boat we go. Lightly row, lightly row. In our boat we go."

Janice settled closer into Dana, already asleep, and put a hand to the wall. She spread her fingers, tapping each one on the wallpaper stippled red and blue. Dot, dot, dotdotdot, she tapped the flecks.

All through their first apartment in Badin, before she and Dana had to come back to this house, Rudy had put battle lanterns along the baseboard. They glowed no bigger than the abdomens of lightning bugs. Five watts each.

"On the ship," he said, "battle lanterns used to be blue. But now they're all red. You see, the navy found out blue could be seen miles up in the sky by a pilot."

"You got to be kidding." Janice held the little bulbs in her hand. "These are just Christmas tree lights, Rudy. Nobody could see these."

"I'm not kidding." Rudy took the red bulbs and stuck them in sockets along the baseboard. "You can see blue all the way up in the sky. So that's why battle lanterns on the ship are red. Every time you get up in the night on the ship, you have to do everything by a red light. We even have to wait in a special room lighted with red lights before we go out on watch."

Janice followed him through their apartment as he put the Christmas tree lights in sockets in the kitchen, the bathroom, and in Dana's room. A red ember under her crib. Dana with an arm hanging through the crib slats.

Janice tapped the wallpaper.

Right now, right this minute, if Rudy Vann got up in the dead of night on the *West Virginia* running fast and hard through a deep mean Pacific Ocean, he had all those red lights to look at.

And if she, Janice, and Dana, too, back in eastern North Carolina, tucked in her family's house, waiting for the new baby to get here, if they had to get up in the night to go to the bathroom or downstairs to the kitchen for a drink of water, they would fall and hurt themselves. This house running fast and hard through the deep mean darkness of North Carolina didn't have any battle lanterns stuck along the baseboard.

Not in one socket anywhere.

"I wish you'd come back, Rudy," Janice whispered. "We'd pinch off lightning bugs and stick them, still lit up, all over the apartment. We'd hang a whole string of Christmas tree lights across the ceiling in the upstairs hall. Look, here."

She rocked, tapping the dots in the wallpaper.

"Before you go on watch at night," Rudy explained, "you sit in this special room with nothing but red lights turned on. And you sit in there and smoke and drink coffee and wait for your eyes to get used to the dark out on deck. There's no light on deck in a battle zone. So you sit in this room in this red light and wait for your eyes to get used to it."

Rudy smiled. "I kind of like that, babe. It's warm, peaceful. Everybody sitting around having a cigarette and a coffee. But then."

He stood up, his voice brisk. "Then you have to go out on watch with that goddamned wool cap scratching the hell out of your ears and that pea jacket rough as a Brillo pad. And you're out there for twelve hours."

Janice drew up her knees close to Dana as best she could with the baby in the way. He is going to be named Rudy the Third, she reminded. Dana's baby brother, and we will write it out *Rudy Vann, III.* It will look good. And we will sign our Christmas cards *Love, Rudy, Janice, Dana and Rudy Vann, III.* It'll look good.

She felt snug and calm as her body heat pulsed from the energy of the baby growing himself bigger and heavier, growing himself, probably, some big blue eyes to stare at them with the day he was born. Janice began to wonder if all that body heat and energy might throw out enough light for a pilot in a plane to see it. Some cruel good-looking man who was their sworn enemy, some Jap or some German, looking for a tender unguarded place to drop a bomb and kill her and Dana Vann and Rudy Vann the Third.

"You can't see us, goddamn you," Janice hissed, shutting her own big blue eyes. "We're asleep. Dead asleep. With the battle lanterns turned off."

Down under Janice and Dana's room, Aunt Zorah in the kitchen was lifting her big red hand to box the ears of Cousin Willie Tatum. Cousin Willie Tatum had been lustily pinching off the coconut frosting from Janice's birthday cake. Down in the basement under the kitchen, deep and thick with little spiders and flying roaches, Uncle Chuck was tasting the scuppernong wine he put up last summer.

Janice Vann hugged Dana and sailed over them all, sleeping the dumbest sleep of her life, and she smiled in her sleep, knowing this whole day, her birthday without Rudy Vann the Second, would never come back again to make her miserable.

"I want you to come back, though, Rudy," she declared one more time. "What'd you want to go to the navy for? Why didn't you just stay in Badin?"

Between the bedroom and the stairs was a long hall, opened on one side like a deck or a balcony, a ship's promenade gallery. At the end of this long hall, the stairs dropped steeply to the empty backyard.

Janice dreamed she woke up in a sweat, her knees cramped and her tongue sore from being clenched between her teeth. Dana still slept in front of her, the hair along her neck damp.

Still hard in the dream Janice slid out of bed, careful not to wake Dana. And careful, too, not to wake Rudy sleeping on his side, snoring a little. Janice slid around Dana, kissing her neck. Rudy snorted as the bedsprings wheezed. He was there all right, just like he never left.

"You sound just like a dog growling, Rudy," Janice chided softly. She wandered through the bedroom, picking up things and putting them back down in the very same place so carefully she never disturbed a single particle of the dust rings around each.

Janice progressed to the upper hall and at once a strong east breeze blew back her hair from her face and pinned her dress against her thick cold body. She hesitated a moment listening, then went straight down the hall, one bare foot before the other, as deliberately and carefully as though measuring off a valuable piece of land.

Janice started down the stairs and she expected them to squeak. When they didn't, she got uneasy and hesitated for the second time, shivering in the strong east breeze that never let up a minute.

At that moment Janice saw Rudy Vann the Second in two places. In the bed she had just left, raised on an elbow, smiling, stroking Dana's head, Dana still asleep. And at the bottom of the stairs, half-turned, waiting and smiling up at her, encouraging her. *Rudy, you're back. You're here!*

At that moment Janice realized the baby she had brought along was so heavy, she couldn't keep on carrying him down the stairs. And she didn't know what to do with him now. She didn't want to throw him away. And it was too late to leave him behind. Put him back up there in the room with Rudy and Dana Vann.

At that moment Janice Vann wanted somebody to help her. But Dana was asleep and everybody downstairs was carrying on about her birthday party, talking loud and banging pots in the kitchen. Rudy, the two Rudys, smiled, a slow half-flicker of muscle in the cheek. Their big blue eyes blazed as blue as Janice's and Dana's eyes, as blue as Rudy the Third's inside Janice could be blazing. In the dark of the empty backyard and the bedroom, their eyes blazed like the blue shards of broken milk of magnesia bottles Janice used to find in the dirt under this same old house.

Rudy asked, reflecting two half-smiles, two sets of blue milk of magnesia bottles, "Where you going, babe?"

They spoke and smiled just like one Rudy: Rudy in her bed and Rudy at the bottom of the stairs.

A quick blue terror charged and held Janice right there on the stairs between the two Rudys.

"You're dead, aren't you, Rudy?" She didn't wait for their smiling answers. "I know you're dead, Rudy."

God, she mourned, some pilot saw the blue lights and dropped a bomb on Rudy Vann the Second. Except it was supposed to be red lights on the ship. Red lights that you can't see up in a plane. But the pilot saw it anyhow and dropped a bomb on Rudy. God, this is the worst thing that's ever happened to me.

"You're not ever coming back now, are you, Rudy?"

For answers, Rudy put his big bare foot on the bottom step. Rudy sat up in the bed beside Dana. Rudy smiled.

"You're supposed to be in the navy," Janice insisted. "Not here on my birthday, Rudy,"

Then she had to sit down all at once and the heavy baby she carried lightened up.

"That's better," she breathed and kissed the top of the baby's head.

He stirred. His feet struck out hard against Janice's ribs, then back up into the blanket. He cried and turned his head, searching for her breast.

"Shh, be quiet, baby," she soothed. "Don't wake up Dana yet. This is just a dream I'm having. And that damn Rudy trying to turn it all into a ghost story."

Trying to get back to her family's house all day long on Janice Vann's birthday, Rudy's ghost didn't have to fight and cut his way through her bad dreams. The briars fell open right in front of his feet, the roses dropped their bright red petals on his sailor cap, and all the thick vines withered back into the dirt along the sides of the porch.

Down in the kitchen under Janice's room, Cousin Willie Tatum yelled when Aunt Zorah's big red hand thwacked the side of his head. Uncle Chuck stumbled up the basement steps, a mason jar of scuppernong wine spilling over his shoes.

"Hey!" he announced to Zorah and Willie Tatum, "this is damn good stuff. I don't care what you say. This is *god!* damn good."

Aunt Zorah let go of Cousin Willie Tatum and pulled out a chair for Uncle Chuck. "Sit," she invited. "I'll cut you some of the birth-day cake I rescued from this glutton who tore into it when my back was turned."

Zorah thwacked a knife through the cake. "*She* won't even come down a minute. *She* won't even say a word. And all I wanted was for her to have a happy birthday and forget about *him.*"

Aunt Zorah rolled her eyes at the ceiling, shook her head. Uncle Chuck sat down. He lined up the mason jar next to the coconut cake. "I knew he wasn't going to come back," he declared. "I told you. I said he was gone for good."

Willie Tatum rubbed his jaw, pulled his ear. "You didn't know nothing," he said. "Neither one of you knows a damned nothing," and he included Aunt Zorah in his scorn.

Upstairs still captured by the bad ghost-dream, Janice Vann examined the baby in her lap. He was crying again, hungry. She held him close as the pillow.

"Where you going, babe?" she soothed. He chuckled, sucked a thumb.

"I bet you want to go downstairs and meet all your folks. It's just Aunt Zorah downstairs and Uncle Chuck and Cousin Willie Tatum. Your folks. And Dana's."

Janice rubbed her eyes, blinked through the shadows. "It's getting dark. Dana will wake up and play with you."

She hugged the baby, hummed in his ear Dana's favorite, "Lightly row, lightly row, in our boat we go."

She tucked his blanket. "How do you like me singing in your ear, babe?"

He yelled at her then and kicked her hard.

Janice Vann woke up for sure, looking around for reassurances, and tried to figure it out for the last goddamned time, *Confound it!*

She was *not* pregnant. Rudy was *not* gone to the navy anymore. *Not* asleep in the middle of the bed with her and Dana. Rudy Vann, the son of a bitch, he had just taken off and left them.

But it *was* her birthday. That much was true. And Janice Vann still wished she had a baby. He would be an old baby now. Rudy Vann the Third. Even *if* Rudy had just taken off and left them like a son of a bitch.

She could still make a hammock for that baby and Dana, something soft and sort of sweaty-smelling out of her arms and breasts, a sailboat *No!* Janice interrupted herself. We don't need a sailboat; we need a goddamned battleship. Get hold of yourself.

Janice's family's house had been asleep for a hundred years in eastern North Carolina, down where the sand was so flat and white, it knocked her eyes out in the middle of the day. There was an enemy pilot in a plane scheduled, she suspected, to fly over every day at the same time and look for the battle lanterns she stuck up.

Janice had changed them all back to blue, five watts each, little strings of Christmas tree lights plugged into every socket she could find. They ought to make a good target, she thought. They ought to light up a goddamned bull's-eye. Then the enemy pilot could drop his bomb and they'd all blow up and this would be over. Rudy would be over.

She shook Dana gently. "Mama," Dana said, scrubbing at her eyes and yawning, "Mama, it's your birthday. What you want?"

Janice smiled. "Dana, what I want is for Rudy Vann, the son of a bitch, to come back and take care of us, me and you and this baby."

"We don't have no baby." Dana frowned. "What baby?"

"This one." Janice hugged him closer. "Rudy Vann the Third." His mouth, she imagined, eased her tight breast, flattened the hard nipple.

"I don't see *no* baby," declared Dana.

"Shh," Janice soothed, "just a dream I'm having."

Out in their sandy bare yard, heavy red roses clawed the sides of the porch, big thorns catching the last light. An enemy plane droned a little closer, and ghosts swarmed like bees to the thick perfume.

OLD HOUSE

They're painting the old kitchen pantry. And the rich paint falls into Chad's eyes and he is blinking and rushing to the sink and running water over his face, blinking more and looking worried and uncertain. Garnet is just standing there scared, not doing a thing to help, watching the water sparkle over Chad's face and shoulders, dart along Chad's big smooth muscles and freckled skin, the water working toward just one thing—to get the burning paint out of his eyes.

"Garnet," he guides, "Garnet," sort of gently hurrying her, groping, "Garnet, where's the damn towel?"

The way he never alarms, the way Chad guides things is something Garnet loves and wants to preserve, the quiet presence, the strong muscles that do not threaten anything.

But here he is with the burning paint in both his eyes, the color she chose for the whole house, everything one soothing unobtrusive color, Antique Satin, a durable luster the Sears label proclaimed, and it is burning Chad.

"Let's paint the doors Chinese red," he first suggested, "the floors jet black." He wanted color, and he spread the color chips across their table like a poker hand.

But she insisted on everything the same Antique Satin, a creamy and gleaming bridal color, perfectly blended and rich as cake. And Chad had agreed and stirred the thick paint in the buckets and rolled it on the wide boards until it splashed in his eyes and burned.

Garnet hands the towel to Chad and he stands up, water still running furiously in the sink, big splashes on the floor, the sparkle of it like ice on the floor. Chad stands up and dabs gently at his eyes. "God," he says, "how in the hell did I do that?"

"Let me see." Garnet looks right into his stinging blue eyes, one with flecks of green, the left eye, and his lashes longer than hers. And she looks and says, "It's gone now, Chad. You got it all. It's all right."

They are in their cutoffs, barefooted, Chad without a shirt, and the old kitchen sultry. A dry hot smell blows in from the pastures and she hears Jasper's cows bellowing from a grove of willows. The house is Jasper's house, and his daddy's house, very old, a century of Jasper's people, their smells in the corners and their hands rubbing the bannister rails smooth.

And Jasper, Chad's daddy, widowed and independent, lives up the road in a smaller house, in one snug room of that house, with central heat and some air-conditioning units plugging the windows.

Then Tierney wakes up and cries across the hall, and Garnet hurries to her. "That scared me, Chad," she calls back, "when the paint got in your eyes." And it had done worse things, the fright clawing right through her like pain. She hated seeing him running water across his face, looking so uncertain, eyes blinking.

"I'm scared," she rocks Tierney, "and when I go back in the kitchen to help Daddy, I'm going to tell him this scared me bad, and I couldn't stand the sight of him blinking that paint, and all the time Jasper's old cows outside bellowing."

The baby's eyes fasten on Garnet like little sponges, soaking up everything in her face, the dark curling of her hair from the heat, the worrying.

"Tierney," Garnet jiggles her, "what you looking at?"

Tierney's eyes soak up everything, then she smiles, lifts a fist with one thumb sticking out as if approving, a baby Roman passing judgment, *Thumbs up, okay.*

"Mama," she mimics, "what you looking at?"

The smell of new paint brightens through the old house with the hot breeze, freshening everything. Garnet kisses Tierney's thumb. "Daddy's painting the house, Tierney, making it look good." And he's killing off the old smells, the old spirits, generations of those old people stuffed up in here for a century. Chad is killing snakes and monsters, room after room. And he's using Antique Satin, durable luster, from Sears. And nothing from a place as dumb as Sears ought to burn a person's eyes out.

She can't let go of the thought—burn a person's eyes out, hurt a person. Maybe the house could kill you, not on purpose, but just because so many things happened in it, because so many people lived in it. Like Jasper's dumb old cows bellowing in the pasture from their grove of green willows, moving around all day, bellowing when they felt like it and startling Garnet anywhere in the house, their mournful cow faces gazing across the fence, through the windows. Like that. Like moving around all day and bellowing like an animal. The old house could jump up and bite you on the leg, throw paint in your husband's eyes, do things.

And then Garnet thinks, well, it's just a dumb old house been in the family forever. Look at it falling apart, not worth the hard work Chad puts in. Still, it has an energy she half admires. The old house scatters itself through two stories and a long ell. To get to their bedroom, Chad and Garnet walk across the long back porch from the old kitchen. To get to the bathroom, they walk across another porch to the other side of the house. These narrow porches built out of wide old-fashioned hand-planed boards, spread inside, outside, upstairs, downstairs, with screens bulging from their frames. And the frames are as fancy as white lace with French curves and spools and lattices.

One room builds into another the way Tierney builds with tinker toys, resulting in elaborate and curious constructions. The walls sweep toward deep ceilings, ten feet high, and a long cool hallway, once a dog-trot, closes in like a big white labyrinth.

And like Tierney's tinker toys, the house looks delicate in places, but holds together. Like the things Tierney makes and then bangs hard on the floor trying to knock them loose. The old house holds together solid as bone.

Overwhelmed by this sprawl of rooms and porches, by doors opening to pantries, clutters of railings and screens, and especially by the steeply pitched tin roof painted a poisonous green, the tin popping like gunshot with each change of the temperature, Garnet is lost. She can't get her bearings. She wants an ordinary suburban ranch house, a plain shell of Sheetrock, one push and it collapses.

Outside big trees, black walnut and pecan, rise up to drop their nuts on the tin roof. *Bang,* the nuts hit, then roll down, clanking in the gutter. Garnet wakes every night there is wind and all the nuts are dropping like bullets. "What?" she gasps, "Chad!"

Chad drowses on his side. "Nothing," he soothes, "nothing."

But she lies there thinking she needs little trees, things as sterile as Bradford pears, shaped and controlled. And a roof of fiberglass.

Two snowball bushes crowd the front steps, growing high as the green gutters, and they throw around their blossoms like careless bridal bouquets, brushing the screens, scattering petals. "It's snowing. It's popcorn." Garnet entertains Tierney, "See, Tierney, it's snowing in the yard. It's snowing popcorn."

Tierney blinks at the snowball bushes. "Snow." The serious vowels echo in her mouth and nose. "Snow."

Garnet watches Tierney's lips form, "Snow," and feels a little dizzy, as if she's just seen God say, "Let there be," and there's no going back. She's got to do something.

In the morning, she watches Chad smear jelly on his toast. "I'm scared in this old house," she tells him, then giggles, feeling silly having said it.

The jelly rises to his mouth, disappears. He smiles. He caps the jar tight. "This old house scares everybody. That's what old houses do, you know that."

He lifts the lid open again, one easy thrust of one big thumb.

"I want to live somewhere else," she says, and takes the jar, rakes a big blob of jelly into her plate. "I want to move to town or something."

Chad watches her fork swirling around in the jelly, smashing butter into the grape. "I'm not making you stay anywhere," he says after awhile. "You can go live anywhere. But I'm staying here. This is our place. Daddy's. Mine and yours. Tierney's."

Garnet doesn't push it. She helps Chad finish painting. The house freshens, becomes less like Jasper's house, more hers, though she still doesn't like it, doesn't trust it.

Jasper walks around one day inspecting. "Y'all done wonders in here," he marvels. "Ain't the same place."

Garnet waits until he finishes looking. Then, "I wish the cows didn't come up so close to the house," she says, "I wish the pasture was a little bit farther off."

Jasper gazes out the living-room windows, tall six-over-six windows. He pats the cream-colored polished cotton she's draped there, the same color as the walls. "I know it," he says. "Them cows is terrible. But that's where it is." She knows he won't do a thing.

And Jasper goes back outside to the cows and the fields and his truck and his snug little modern house up the road. He's not worrying. He knows exactly where he is. Garnet feels ashamed of herself. And then gets irritated.

Late that afternoon, right after Chad comes in from work, Tierney falls all the way down the old stairs and lands in a soft heap. For a moment, Garnet can't move, thinking Tierney is dead. Then the soft heap gathers itself, pulls all its breath to one place, and hollers. Tierney is okay, hollering and hollering, and when Garnet finally picks her up, she has to sink back down again on the bottom step, her knees are so weak.

"Let me see her," Chad tries to take the baby, but Garnet pulls Tierney closer, shakes her head fiercely at Chad.

"She's okay," Garnet hisses at him. "She fell all the way down the stairs, but she's okay."

She's amazed how much she enjoys keeping Tierney from Chad. At how effectively she prevents him from comforting Tierney. At how Chad just lets her do it, just stands there while Tierney hollers.

Jasper has run in from the yard and he, too, has to stand and look on while Garnet holds Tierney to her own body and hugs her and Tierney hollers louder.

After awhile, Jasper says, "If you go get a silver knife and hold it to her head where she bumped it, it will make the swelling go down and won't leave no big bruise."

Chad scoffs softly, "A silver knife, Daddy?"

"You try it," insists Jasper. "Go back in the kitchen and get a silver knife and hold it to her head."

When Chad comes back with the silver knife, Garnet lets go of Tierney just enough for him to put it against her head. Tierney stops hollering and stares at her father. "What that thing?" she asks.

"A silver knife," he soothes, "to make Tierney okay."

"Yes," affirms Jasper, "a silver knife to make my baby okay." He moves in closer, encouraged. "Them mean old stairs hurt my baby and I'm going to spank them old stairs." He smacks the stair steps. "See, Tierney, I spanked them old stairs for hurting my baby. Now they going to cry."

And Jasper wrinkles up his old face and boo-hoos. Tierney grins, laughs out loud at him. "Them mean old stairs," she mimics, "now they going to cry."

Chad has eased down beside Garnet on the bottom step, still holding the silver knife to Tierney's head. Garnet feels herself relax as soon as Chad gets close. After awhile she lets him take the baby on his lap. Tierney and Chad appear to be perfectly blended, she thinks, like paint, like blood. Tierney pats the knife on her forehead and Chad pats Tierney.

Jasper tromps down the back porch and Garnet follows. He opens the screen door and before he steps through, he seems to study something off in the pasture, the clumps of cows, the salt blocks stuck on low poles.

"You really want that pasture moved back?"

"Yes," Garnet brightens, "yes, please. It comes up too close to the house. I see cow faces looking in at all the windows."

Jasper chuckles, changes the subject. "One time Chad's mama got so mad at me, she took every dish off the supper table in yonder." Jasper hikes a shoulder toward the kitchen. "Took every dish off the supper table and marched out to them black walnut trees and busted every one."

He pauses again, studying something way off. "I went out there and looked at all them busted dishes and I said, 'You feel better now?'"

Garnet imagines all the broken plates and cups under the walnut trees. She wonders why Jasper tells her this stuff. She suspects it has something to do with her and the pasture, with the whole place, maybe even with Tierney falling down the stairs. She interrupts, "Where was Chad?"

Jasper blinks, gathers up his attention, "Chad won't even born."

Now in the night, when walnuts hit the tin roof, Garnet dreams plates and cups are crashing overhead. "Chad," she says half asleep, sounding out Jasper's syllables, "you won't even born."

Jasper moves the pasture back ten feet along the west side of the old house, straining in the hot sun, pulling up the stout cedar posts and reseating them, tightening the barbed wire. Garnet watches and approves. Then feels as terrified as she did when Chad got the paint in his eyes. It's the power she has, the things she can get them to do, Chad and Jasper. It's the old house, she thinks, the years and years of women busting up dishes. Blinding a man with paint, throwing a baby down the stairs, working a man to death in the hot sun.

She waits to see Jasper keel over dead, the cows licking his face, tramping his cedar posts and his wire. But Jasper is tough, hard and dry as leather. He gets the whole west side of the house free for Garnet. No more cow faces looking in the windows at her.

"I'm taking the calves off tomorrow," he warns her, throwing tools in the truck. "You and Chad's going to hear some hollering."

And he is right. As soon as their calves are gone, the cows crowd the pasture fences, hollering and bawling all day and into the hot fragrant night. It doesn't matter that the fences are back now ten feet. Cow faces are everywhere Garnet looks. And their bawling is pitiful.

"Why do they keep on doing that?" she complains to Chad. "They're just cows."

Chad smiles, his eyes as sweet as fresh air. "That's why," he says, "they're just poor old cows."

They bellow through the night and toward dawn, a big storm explodes over the house. Garnet and Chad both wake up and watch the lightning. Everything outside floods, and the big trees whipping in the wind, the cow faces at the fences are illuminated in startling clear bursts. Rain pours off the tin roof, walnuts tumbling like bowling pins. Garnet thinks Tierney is crying across the hall. "You hear that?" she pulls at Chad. "You hear Tierney. She's probably scared."

Garnet is afraid to get out of bed and put her bare feet on the old smooth floor, afraid the lightning will strike. She wants to go to Tierney, and thinks of her standing in the crib, ducking close to the bars when the lightning cracks. *Oh, Tierney.* Garnet wants to comfort Tierney with something solid and reliable, give Tierney something she can hold in her hands for a hundred years, years after she, Garnet, is dead.

She wants to get up and go do this, but thunder barrels overhead and she flinches.

"I'll go check on her." Chad slides out of bed and is gone like a shadow. Gone before Garnet can say another word, think another thought. Gone to rescue Tierney, bring her back to their bed and cover her with their sheet, crowd her in between their bodies for the length of the storm.

And while she waits, Garnet begins to see in the flashing light and darkness something like a long twisting telescope of years. Years and years all stuck together like Tierney's tinker toys. Garnet only imagines this, but it is so real, her breath catches and her throat tightens. She sees down to the year her husband might die and she might walk in to find him through such a storm as this one, the cows bawling outside and the walnuts pelting. She might walk in on bare feet, the old floors still holding solid. Walk in and find him dead at fifty, at sixty, at seventy, his calm blue eyes fixed on something behind her, way off in the distance.

Chad is studying something. He doesn't even know she's there, and it hurts her worse than anything in her whole life. "Chad," she whispers, "Chad, it's okay. It's just the poor old cows outside bawling for the calves. And it's lightning and it's your mama's dishes breaking on the roof like Jasper told me, Chad. It's okay."

He doesn't answer, doesn't even turn to look at her. Just keeps studying something way off in the flashing and echoing distance.

And then Garnet starts crying, as wildly as the hard rain flooding across the tin roof, cries for herself alone in that bed in that big old house, cries until Chad returns with Tierney in his arms and fixes a place between them both.

Tierney sits up there looking around, delighted, her hair like a dark cloud, her nostrils flaring gently, and then she reaches one finger and collects the glossy tears on Garnet's face like dotting crumbs on a plate. "Mama," she observes, "crybaby, crybaby."

Garnet feels, like a pleasant breath, the house and all its years settling around the three of them in the wild rain. Feels the house settling like a skin, something as familiar as her own face, something as natural and determined as Tierney's finger. And the smell of the house is evergreen, a gaudy perennial flower, long-lived, for good.

INFANTICIDES

The group forms:

Dan, the big brother, gets an apartment. Out of nowhere, Cathleen, the curious and disturbed girl, joins him. Then Waverly, the little brother, comes up to Chapel Hill to enter the School of Business and take accounting just like Dan. They call him Wave. "Here's Wave. Wave's here." Waverly likes it when they call him Wave, makes him feel a welcome part of the group. He watches them and learns and wants to be everything they are and acquire their tastes.

Cathleen herself is an acquired taste, a fragrant seizure, exotic and sudden. She disappears weeks at a time, then shows up drunk at the front door. Dan drags her to the bathroom, Waverly runs the water, Dan strips her, then into the tub, and Cathleen lies there, her hair turning limp in the steam, her shoulders glistening. The Ivory soap bobs at her breast and she slaps it to the other end of the tub. "I love you all," she proclaims, "I love everybody in this apartment. You, too, Wave."

Then they put Cathleen to bed.

For a few days, maybe a month, she is okay, agreeable and cheerful, fitting into some sort of unspoken schedule with Dan. Waverly hasn't figured it out yet, but likes to watch. Dan and Cathleen know how to get through life, he thinks. They know the truth about things, what matters.

Cathleen isn't a student at Carolina, she doesn't work anywhere in Chapel Hill, she's not in love with Dan and he's not in love with Cathleen. The sex they share is as perfect as an accounting problem, gets worked out, no mess, the right answers every time. And it plainly awes Waverly. It's because I'm younger, he tells himself.

He thinks he might be a little in love with Cathleen.

Cathleen isn't pretty. Her best attribute is her hair, straight as a stick and when they wash it for her, it is the most colorful hair Waverly ever saw, amber and honeyish, touched with rich darks and sudden lights, some of them tending toward red.

If she feels especially good, Cathleen calls herself a strawberry blonde. Waverly says no, strawberry is not the right word for that wonderful splash of hair. And when he catches himself dreaming about Cathleen, it is always her hair, long and vibrant, dirty or clean, wet or dry, hanging right in front of him. Waverly reaches for it in his dream, and the grasping of it, the feeling of it all over him, is as energetic and jubilant as sex. Cathleen despises the pale lashes and brows setting off her brown eyes, so she puts sooty mascara on her lashes and brows and it streaks off, leaving her with a raccoon look made more garish by the bright perfumy lipstick she prefers.

Still, with a good skin, no freckles or scars, Cathleen appears to Waverly unblemished. He thinks that with the mascara wiped off, the lipstick gone, Cathleen is a highly desirable woman.

She walks around the apartment naked and Dan sleeps naked, but the minute he gets out of bed, he pulls on underwear or jeans or whatever comes to hand. If anybody comes in before he gets dressed, Dan jumps for a towel or tries to cover up with a magazine, hollering, "Damnit! Can't you *knock?*"

Waverly feels like a piece of furniture those times when Cathleen walks around naked, her breasts bobbing over her ribs. If she is having her period, she still walks around naked, but with bikini panties on, the tampon string sometimes trailing out, and then Dan has a real fit.

"Put on some clothes," he yells. "Show some *modesty!*"

Cathleen just lights a cigarette and grins and rolls her eyes. Cathleen doesn't care, she doesn't care if Dan hollers at her, or if Waverly watches.

"Look, Wave," she says. "When a woman's been treated good, it shows in her face. Look here at my face. Looks good, right?"

She is right. Smooth, with no freckles, no scars, curiously unblemished, every part of her face and body is smooth and undisturbed. Even those times when Cathleen shows up at the door after a long bivouac, drunk, there won't be a mark on her, no bruise or scratch to disturb that smoothness.

"Right, Cathleen," Waverly smiles.

"Wave," she continues, stroking her hair, "okay, you better treat women good, so that it shows in their face. Now, let me kiss you."

She plants him a fragrant smudgy kiss, her breasts brushing across his Carolina blue sweatshirt. She kisses Waverly like the little brother. A few evenings or hours later, when he hears, in the next room, Cathleen enter eagerly into wild vigorous sex with Dan, the memory of the smudgy kiss disturbs Waverly.

They play tennis a lot that spring. Dan is good on the courts, Cathleen and Waverly lob along less than fair, but fair enough to keep Dan going, one after the other. So sometimes they play for hours, then knock off for beer. One hot May Saturday a baby is parked in a pram near the courts. Its parents are playing tennis, but they don't appear too concerned about this baby, rarely stopping to check on it. Likewise, the baby doesn't seem to miss them, waving its fists in the air, holding one still a minute as if inspecting it, then waving both about again.

Cathleen notices right off. At the first break in her game with Dan, she goes over to look at the baby waving its fists. The baby stops a minute and stares at her, then goes back to waving its fists. She says nothing, but as the afternoon progresses, she goes back and looks at the baby again and again. She even puts in her hand to let the baby grasp a finger, then laughs and tugs her finger back. She asks the parents what's its name.

"Rollo," they pant, wiping sweat from their faces.

"Rollo? That's not a name for a baby." Cathleen shakes her head. "That's *his* name." The parents, satisfied she is harmless, go back to the courts.

"Rollo." Cathleen studies him as intently as he studies his fists. "Rollo. Those jerks named you Rollo."

So far as Waverly can see, it's just a big old bald red-faced baby dumped like a pig in the shade of its pram at the side of the courts. "What's going on with Cathleen and that baby?" he asks Dan, feeling a little jealous.

"Nothing," Dan spits, wipes his face. "Nothing."

After awhile, though, it plainly annoys Dan the way she keeps going back to look at the baby, giving it her finger to grab. He stops the game, stalks off the courts, and when they follow him, Dan hisses, "I like to play tennis with people who play back."

Cathleen leans against the fence, a breeze ruffling her hair. She folds both arms and looks down at them, sort of smiling into her arms as she had into the baby's pram. "I play with babies, if I want to."

"You like to make trouble, if you want to."

Cathleen lifts her head, smiles hard at Dan, "If I want to."

Disgusted, Dan snorts and bangs his racket on the fence, "Shut up."

"What's going on?" Waverly asks.

"Nothing," Cathleen shrugs away from them both, "nothing."

And since something obviously is going on and they won't say what, a little hairline fracture suddenly loosens the solid picture he has of his brother and Cathleen.

Cathleen straightens up. "Do you like babies, Wave?" she challenges, ignoring Dan. "Did you like that baby back there?" She hikes a perfect and tanned shoulder toward the pram.

"Stop it," warns Dan.

"Make me." Cathleen twirls her racket. "Make me."

They go back to the apartment, picking up more beer on the way, and Cathleen gets drunk and belligerent and they bathe her and put her to bed in Dan's room and try to make her go to sleep, but she won't. She keeps on talking, talking, talking, and then looking at Waverly, demands, "Wave, when you get married, will you have a bunch of babies?"

She doesn't wait for his answer, but rushes on to challenge Dan, "What about you? When you get married, will you have a bunch of babies?"

Dan exhales dramatically, "I don't know. It depends."

"On what?" she presses.

"On whether or not I love the person."

"Explain." Cathleen's brown eyes narrow like an animal's, the dissolving mascara making her look wildly raccoon-eyed.

"I ought not to even talk to you," says Dan. "I ought not to even argue with you, Cathleen, when you get like this."

He walks around his room, adjusting the blinds. They clatter against the windows, swag sideways. "If I love the person," he continues, "I'll have kids. If I don't love her, I won't."

Waverly interrupts in spite of himself. "Excuse me but why get married in the first place if you don't love the person?"

Dan hesitates, then takes on a kind of lecturing tone, "You can love her when you get married and then not love her after awhile." He jerks the blinds trying to level them. "It all depends.

"Oh, Jesus." Cathleen closes her raccoon eyes. "It all depends. It all *depends*," she mimics Dan, and then turning toward Waverly and opening her eyes, mimics him, "Excuse *me*, excuse *me.*"

She begins crying, the raccoon mascara running straight down both cheeks, looking, to Waverly, sillier than ever, and also more bitter.

Dan won't tolerate the tears and he recoils as though Cathleen has thrown up on him. "I want you to shut up, now, Cathleen, I know where you're going with this conversation and I want you to shut up now."

Cathleen has never cried in front of Waverly before and he feels disappointed in her, and almost jealous, the same way he had felt about her attentions to the bald red baby at the tennis courts.

Then Cathleen gets quiet, blinking her tears. She scrubs her face, her lashes now pale and free from the mascara, her breath calming, calming, slowing. And after several minutes of intense and threatening quiet, a crazy horrifying little story spills out of her, getting crazier and more horrifying as she goes along.

She talks about a baby she had when she was thirteen and took him out in the backyard and buried him. She dug a hole in the dirt. *"Look!"*

Cathleen's hands are straight in front of her and she spreads her fingers apart and claws at the bedspread. Her nails glint like red glass over the little tufts of chenille.

"I dug a hole in the dirt and covered him up." She begins to pat the chenille, hard, harder, and talks about how she put dirt in his mouth and dirt in his nose and held both her hands over his face, too.

She makes coarse brutal sounds, blaming people because they knew what she was doing in the backyard. "Wave," she insists, "they were watching and not one of them stopped me. Not a single son-of-a-bitching one."

"For God's sake, Cathleen, shut up," Dan mutters behind Waverly.

"That's right, shut up," Cathleen relaxes, "shut up." Her hair floods out, still wet from the bath, still fragrant with Ivory soap. She appears to quieten a moment, blinks, then addresses herself entirely to Waverly.

"Wave, you know what I liked about that baby named Rollo today at the tennis court?"

Waverly feels his mouth hanging open, feels stupid and feeble, and hates himself and also Dan and Cathleen for making this scene, yet he tamely asks her, "What?"

"He was looking at his hands. Yes." Cathleen makes fists, holds them up and studies them, mimicking the baby's stare. Her fists tighten, relax, tighten again. "I liked that, Wave."

Dan, glowering in a corner, lights a fresh cigarette and offers it to Cathleen to shut her up. "Don't live through it again, Cathleen," he orders, "shut up, go to sleep, you're drunk."

Waverly feels like a baby, stuffed with dirt and buried alive, his mouth and his nose numbed, stupid and vulnerable as the bald, red-faced baby named Rollo.

Cathleen falls back, still scratching at the chenille. "Cold premeditated murder. That's what they called it."

"That's what it was," affirms Dan, "you did it. You knew you did it."

"Cold premeditated murder." Her skin darkened from the crying looks blotchy. "I was thirteen," Cathleen says. "Do you know what would happen if I did it now?"

Nobody answers.

"If I did it now, they'd give me the gas chamber. But I was thirteen, so they gave me a light sentence."

She snorts. "Locked me up."

"I can't stand anymore of this," Dan knocks the bed, "Cathleen. Every time you get drunk, you do this," and he turns Waverly toward the door and shuts the door hard behind them both.

Waverly goes into the kitchen behind Dan, feeling betrayed and self-righteous. "What in the hell was all that?"

"I don't know," Dan shrugs irritably, "Cathleen's drunk."

"Did she really kill it?"

"I don't know," Dan insists, his voice growing more irritable. "She says she did. It's her business. Forget it."

"Look, Dan." Waverly balls a fist first at him, then back at the bedroom door. "I don't want to forget it." He half rises from the chair, "I want to know all about it. Everything you know, Dan."

Dan gazes at Waverly for a long time while the kitchen linoleum pops and water gurgles in the drain, then he lights a cigarette, and after a deep draw says in a tone full of pity and impatience, "Wave, it's Cathleen's business. And like I said, forget it."

Waverly studies this for the rest of the evening and he promises himself, *In the morning, I will get to the bottom of this, in the morning, I will look Cathleen straight in the face and ask her, soon as she gets up.*

And after awhile, he realizes that it is not Cathleen killing a baby that shocks him, but the fact that Dan knew it and never told him. He realizes he doesn't care about the killing. He only cares about being told, being taken into the group and told all the secrets, told everything Dan and Cathleen know. And when he gets this firmly fixed in his head, Waverly is ashamed. And fascinated by his shame.

I will ask Cathleen in the morning, he assures himself. *Cathleen will explain all this.*

But in the morning, Cathleen is still asleep when he leaves for class, and in the afternoon when he gets back, Cathleen is gone. And Dan is leafing through the paper, whistling, reading about people killing people off cold, people breaking people's hearts, and nobody saying a word, the place full of mindless perfection, all the numbers working out, accounted for.

They can't do this to me anymore, thinks Waverly, *I won't be the little brother anymore.*

"Listen, Dan," he dumps his books on the floor, pulls out a chair, "where's Cathleen?"

Dan turns a page, eyes him, turns another page, "Gone," he says, "like always."

"Just like that!" Waverly snaps his fingers. "She shows up when she feels like it, when you feel like it. The two of you fuck each other to death and then everybody's happy, and then she gets gone when she feels like it, when you feel like it, too. Just like that! And you don't tell me anything and we carry on around here like nothing. Just like *that!*"

Dan throws down the paper as Waverly snaps his fingers the third time, and then he advances to Waverly's chair. "Look, Wave," he mutters through his teeth, "what do you want?"

"I want you to tell me things," Waverly clenches his teeth just like Dan. "I want you to feel sorry."

Dan studies him awhile, then, "Cathleen doesn't need me to feel sorry," he declares. "Or you," he adds in a voice so flat and so final, Waverly knows there is no more argument. The story is over. He will have to take Cathleen just the way Dan does, the way she takes herself, showing up, going off again, a final accounting, the right answer, genuine perfection, and nothing matters so long as the numbers come out right.

He sits there a little longer, hoping Dan will look up from the paper again and when he doesn't, Waverly kicks his books aside and heads into the bathroom. He intends to make a lot of noise, turning on the water wide open, slinging stuff around.

It's so quiet and humid, with such a thick fragrance of Ivory sticking to the tub, Waverly thinks he could scrape it off with a blade, the soap and the silence. And there, too, twisting from the faucet, catching what faint light struggles through the blinds, is one of Cathleen's long red hairs, dry as an insect.

He turns on the hot water, making the pipes shiver and rumble, stirring the water as hard as he can and hating the Ivory smell that rises with the rich suds. Then he undresses and slides in and he begins to plan how he will acquire tastes for the plainest things in life, the blandest and cleanest and smoothest women with nothing in their faces that might jump out and hit him, no red hair down their backs. And these women, Waverly declares, will major in accounting, carry abacuses to bed and zing the beads up and down the wires, perfect.

THE OTHER SIDE
OF THE WORLD

Years after she stopped sleeping with her twin, Willy still wanted him in the bed with her. Still felt Kep all over her, giggling and growling, and that hot rush spreading and spreading like a silly grin, and no way to stop.

So you fucked your brother, or maybe you thought you did, so what. Okay. Here's what, she kept explaining and explaining, telling it like a big story she invented to amuse herself, a big movie she starred herself in. Telling it, finally, to her husband, Marshall Bell, who said, well, there's worse things and it's what kids do all the time and who cares.

And so it wasn't just wanting to sleep with Kepley again, like kids, or confessing that she used to do this that obsessed her. But also getting mad at Marshall, or at anybody else she told, when they didn't believe her or pay enough attention, getting mad and obsessed enough to kill them, gun them right down.

And Shura, the little girl, standing there, too, in big-eyed innocence, watched her get mad at Marshall. Feeling Willy rush right past her to the bedroom, ignore her, push Shura away.

"What that?" Shura pointed at the wall, reaching one hand to grab at Willy, but Willy rushed by too fast.

Then Marshall coming from the living room, coming from the light and comfort of their big soft living room with cushions and the open April windows, coming into the narrow dark hall to rescue Shura.

Shura caught between the living room and Willy's bedroom.

But Shura, stubborn as Willy, kept on standing there on short bare legs, a finger wet from her mouth, and her face packed to the brim with anxiety, asked Marshall:

"What that? What that might be?" pointing the wet finger at something on the dark knotty pine wall.

An old bear, Shura. Your old bear mother.

Willy didn't care. She piled up in her bedroom, even knowing Shura was scared of that knotty pine wall, and even knowing she could set Shura free from the beast, she stayed in middle of the bed. Selfish, aren't you? Real selfish. I'm sorry, Shura. I'm sorry you have to take it right in the middle of the hall all by yourself, and I don't care enough to get up off the bed and come help.

"What, honey?" Marshall. Light floated over his solid figure. Willy smelled the strong, fresh outdoors smell off him. Good smell. Straight and to the point. Light and the outdoors spread off Marshall, along with his Salem Menthol, filled the hall, and pushed into the bed beside Willy. She rolled away.

"What?"

Shura pointed at the knotty pine. "What that might be?" she asked again.

Marshall squatted down, lifted Shura and settled her on his knee, then guided her wet finger around the dark whorl. "Nothing, honey. Just the wall. See?"

He traced the knotty pine again with Shura's finger on his. Then he patted her bare legs, took her back into the April light with him.

Willy turned her face to the dark whorled wall of her own room. She wanted the light and the sun and good smells, wanted Marshall and Shura. How did this get started? Shit, she reminded herself, you like it, like to hurt people. And you already know how it got started.

Willy wanted to tell it to somebody, all the way back. Shura, honey, come here, up here on my bed with me, and let's roll around and giggle, and let me tell you things.

Willy rubbed her own wet fingers over the thick coverlet, True Lover's Knot, knot, knot. Each thread holding fast in strong woolen homespun, and her heart beating like crazy, and her grief spreading, tightening and worsening, holding together like stitches over a deep bloody cut, tightening and going hard, scabbing over. The old bear in the knotty pine is the old bear in the coverlet. It's me, and it's Kepley, and it's you, too, Shura.

Listen to what I'm saying. Listen to this story:

When they were still nothing but twin children in Badin, North Carolina, Willy slept in the same bed with Kepley because that was easier and they both liked it and their mother, Evelyn Smith, didn't think anything about it. Instead of listening to bedtime stories, Willy wanted to act things out. She wanted everybody to sit down and watch her act and dance, too, especially dance. And Willy danced, turned, and kept spinning until Evelyn said, "Stop, you're getting me dizzy. Rest a minute."

Kepley pitched a fit, sprawled in the middle of their bed, one leg dangling over the side.

"Don't look at her," he bossed Evelyn. "Go on and read the book. *Read!*"

"In a minute," Evelyn swatted his leg. "Just shut up and watch Willy a minute. Let me clear my head from all that turning around and around she's doing."

Willy put her hands over her head and started spinning again, her cotton nightgown filling with plain old Badin air over her ankles, spin, spin, I'll make you drunk and dizzy, make you fall down.

"I'm a balloon, a balloon," she directed herself. "No, a cocoon, a cocoon! Watch me float on off from here. Or bust open and turn into a butterfly."

"I'll bust you," Kep snorted.

"No," Willy struck a pose, brought her hands down, flexed a knee. She put a finger in the corner of each eye and pulled both back in a slant to gaze at Kepley. Then, spinning again, mocked him.

"Look, here's a girl who had a brother she beat up every day, and she had teeth (here Willy clacked her teeth together) and bit him on the leg, and had some sharp claws and stripey fur and slanty eyes (here Willy pulled her eyes back more), and she jumped on him in the dark, and beat him up so bad he couldn't do a thing, either."

"Listen!" Kep pointed at her, then glared at Evelyn, "Did you hear that big fat lie she just told! I'll beat you up, Willy!" and he banged his leg against the bed, and sat up, both fists ready.

"Shut up." Evelyn swatted him again. "Let your sister finish this."

Willy stopped spinning. The swirls of cotton settled softly around her, little faded hands of cotton patting her knees, her thighs. "I'm finished," she said, and climbed into bed beside Kep.

"Go on, read," they both directed Evelyn.

"I'm too tired," she complained. "You all wear me out. Why don't you two just lie here and squawk at each other."

"No!" they demanded. "Read us a story!"

"No," she said, "shut up. This is it. No more."

And later, the light out, and Evelyn gone, Kepley hissed, "That was your fault. All you ever do is show off, and wear people out."

Willy kicked him. "I don't care."

"All you ever do is get people to look at you." He kicked her back hard.

She rolled against Kep and they wrestled over the dark warm rumpled bed.

"You're so dumb," he said again, holding her fast with his hard legs, scratching her with his rough boy's toenails that Evelyn cut square across the ends. "You're such a show-off."

"I don't care if I am." Willy pounded him, pulled at his ears. "I don't care a thing I do."

And they fell asleep, arms and legs tangled. In the morning, when Willy woke up, Kepley would be gone, and she felt a part of herself gone, too, a tingling memory in her legs and arms where other arms and legs had been, stronger arms, harder and tougher and longer legs with rough toenails.

Willy rolled across the double bed, wrapping her arms around herself, wanting those missing parts back, yet despising them a little at the same time. Despising herself for wanting them. Those parts, Kep's parts, knew where they were going and knew how to get what they wanted and didn't have to act out anything, or dance around in a cotton nightgown, and didn't have to make up stories to get people to look.

This is Willy, she told the sheets, the lumps and hollows of the pillows. She kissed the places Kep had punched. Slanty eyes. Fur, and long sharp claws, too, and teeth to bite him on the leg.

This is Willy, she told the yellow chenille spread. She spread apart the tufts Kep had pinched. Kepley doesn't even know this is the real Willy.

Later, Willy made up a handsome blond and tanned woman she called Wolfsheena, and tried to share her with her best friend in Badin, Frances Murdoch. But Frances was too bored and tamed, maybe too satisfied, to catch on to something like Wolfsheena. Wolfsheena, the perfect dark companion, a twin to rival Kepley, Wolfsheena, with Willy's teeth and her claws. Wolfsheena did the dancing and told all the stories. Showed off good. ·

"This is Wolfsheena," she taunted Kepley.

"Who's that, somebody like Tarzan?" he sneered.

"Better than Tarzan." Willy spun around, jumped on a cushion, struck an arabesque.

"Nothing's better than Tarzan," said Kepley. "Unless it's Zorro."

Zorro, Zorro, yes, Zorro, too. And the dark slanty-eyed Wolfsheena. Kepley didn't know the twin he had. Willy wasn't sure herself. Wolfsheena was as unsatisfactory, sometimes, as the empty bed the next morning.

She and her brother were Willoughby and Kepley Smith, Jimmie Smith's twins, born in Badin where Jimmie Smith ran the only drugstore.

Bishop LeGrande, older than Badin and anybody else in it, used to come in the drugstore and say, "Gimme some fountain water, Mr. Jimmie, with some ice."

And after sipping and crunching thoughtfully a moment, Bishop LeGrande declared to everybody in there, "Ain't it sad the way life turns out."

It wasn't a question Bishop wanted answered. It was a declaration he wanted agreed to. And everybody in the drugstore agreed, "Yes, sad, sad."

Some days he gazed wonderingly at Willy and Kep, both of them twirling on the soda fountain stools, and he declared, "Black folks don't have no twin chirrun. Not much, anyway. I don't recall in my life knowing no black twin chirrun around here."

Bishop shook his head, correcting himself. "Except for them two Meachum boys. You know, Mr. Jimmie, they stayed over at Charlotte. But they was all messed up. Was all pinky-looking, even their eyes."

"Albinos," said Jimmie Smith.

"I don't know what you call it. But they wasn't real folks." Bishop wiped his black wrinkled face, his face that gleamed from tree trunks in the landscapes of Willy's night stories, his face that melted and reformed its knowing grin on the black alligators Wolf-sheena danced over, their old hungry teeth waiting for a leg, a square-cut toenail.

Bishop wiped his face on his sleeve, declared, "Ain't it sad the way life turns out."

"I want a Coke." Kep smacked the counter. "I want a Coke with *vanilla* in it."

"What do you want, Willy?" Her daddy leaned over her and smiled. His breath was rich, and Willy liked it, Lucky Strikes, coffee, Dentine.

"I want the same thing," she smiled back.

Bishop LeGrande occupied a dark hard place in Willy's family. He had always been around in Badin, always part of the Smiths, tenacious and undeniable, especially devoted to her grandmother. An old black man who came with the deal, on the house, so to speak, pronouncing truths, whether anybody asked him or not.

When they visited their grandmother on Sunday afternoons, there sat Bishop LeGrande on the screened back porch, in a sunny splotch of January sun, warming himself alongside his wife, Orrie.

Or they rested like two dark presences in the thick green August shade stretching out of the big oaks rearing all around the roof.

Orrie hardly said a word, but waggled her black fingers at Willy and Kep, grinning and coaxing. Her teeth were spangled with gold. Willy never saw wealthy teeth like that in any other person's mouth until she saw Marshall's mouth. Marshall Bell who always wanted to talk about family trees and where she came from and what kind of ancestors she had, especially what stories she had heard about them. Marshall Bell who loved her in a way that never left the bed empty, and whom Willy loved back and had Shura with, and then she, Willy, tormented them both, Shura and Marshall.

Marshall never had anybody in his life like Bishop and Orrie.

Willy wanted to give both Bishop and Orrie to Marshall, to make him laugh and see the gold flash in his teeth. She first made up stories for him, and acted out the parts of Bishop and Orrie. Then she showed him the real Bishop and Orrie in Badin. And she showed him, too, her real teeth and claws.

On their Grandmother Smith's back porch, Bishop again often took long wondering gazes at Willy and Kep, shaking his head and teasing, "How'd you get two chirrun on one shot, Mr. Jimmie?"

Orrie cackled and shoved him.

"And two different kinds," Bishop added. "*Two* different kinds!"

If Evelyn Smith heard Bishop LeGrande, she would retort without hesitation, "I can tell you how you get two on one shot. It's really easy, just *too* easy."

But it wasn't easy. She lied about it. Willy listened to her mother complain and elaborate about their gestation and delivery so much, she could imagine how it all took place from the moment of their conception in Badin. She imagined she lay transversal and heavy on top of Kepley, who curled in proper cephalic presentation in Evelyn's lower pelvis. Willy jumped and jerked against Evelyn's ribs, pushing for room. But Kepley took his time, serene and cunning, planning things. He already knew how to take advantage.

They lay that way for nearly nine and a half months until Evelyn said, "This is just damned ridiculous. I don't believe in babies, anyhow."

She threw out her hands, gave up, annoyed with the whole slow process, declaiming all over the house with every gesture exaggerated, "I don't even know, Jimmie, how come I'm going around looking like this, all pooched out, looking worse than hell itself, hardly able to walk. Damn it all, Jimmie, I can't even draw a decent breath, and it's your fault."

"Well, you asked for it, Evelyn. Quit bitching."

"Asked for it! Asked for it!" She kicked the wall.

Jimmie Smith gave up, too. He hauled her to the hospital twice on false alarms, then started sleeping in the guest room. Evelyn quit sleeping altogether, and started sitting up all night in a big wing chair. Later, she would sit in the same chair and nurse the babies, propping her arms and their heads and her enormous breasts on its richly colored bird-in-a-bower brocade.

Willy imagined she spoke to Kepley by that time. But he ignored her in his hateful superior way, his all-knowing way. Kepley ignored the whole outside fuss and bother, keeping himself all curled and closed up in there, warm as pie, his fists under his chin, his feet soft as red shadows.

Willy got really mad at him then, and hissed, "Well, the least you could do is get the hell out of the way!"

Because if he had gotten out of the way, Willy could have slipped on out of Evelyn and been born. And Kep could have stayed curled inside of Evelyn as long as he liked. Kepley couldn't be bargained with. Willy was ready weeks before their birthday, but Kepley kept on waiting, smooth and peaceful and superior, content to be where he was, taking advantage of Evelyn and Jimmie and her.

Then in late October 1941, when the moon had filled to a great white bowl over Badin, Kep moved. And Willy followed, bigger than he at birth, and longer and heavier. She wasn't the first to get out. Smaller and quieter, all-knowing, her brother led their way out of Evelyn's hot red innards. He was as sure as a little compass, as aimed as a bullet, and he knew exactly where they were going, the both of them.

He knew more than Evelyn. When she felt the first pains, she didn't bother to wake up Jimmie in the guest room. Evelyn thought it was another false alarm, and she couldn't stand to get in another fight about that. But she called up Doctor Lapsley, just on the chance that the babies might really mean it this time. Doctor Lapsley advised, "We can't take any chances, Evelyn. But don't wake up Jimmie. Just get ready, and I'll come by in a minute and take you to the hospital."

She packed her suitcase, the one she and Jimmie Smith shared, a scratched black cowhide with the scruffy decals of Natural Bridge, Virginia, the Washington Monument, and Glen Echo. And she took along in a little paper bag the two white dresses for Willy and Kepley.

"Those are the two smallest dresses I could find," she later told Grandmother Smith, the day they dressed the twins to bring back home. "And still they're too big. Look."

Willy's arm disappeared in a sleeve. Kep's chin dropped behind the little collar.

"It doesn't matter, Evelyn," said their grandmother. "They don't know what they've got on."

Evelyn packed her suitcase and took along the paper bag. Doctor Lapsley took her to the hospital, and the twins were born as Kepley arranged. Jimmie Smith didn't know anything until the next morning.

"I was sleeping good," he loved to tell, "and the phone rang, and Doctor Lapsley said, 'How many twins you got at your house?' "

He loved to tell this at the drugstore when new parents came in to buy formula pitchers and Curity cotton balls. He flicked the ash off his Lucky Strike, totaled the costs of Pablum and cod liver oil.

" 'Well, I don't have any twins at my house,' I said. 'Well, you got some now,' he said. And I got over to the hospital as fast as I could, and when I saw Kep and Willy, I could hardly believe it."

Hardly anybody believed it. Everybody was glad it was over because Evelyn had been such a bitch the last months, not able to walk around without knocking against the wall or the door, not able to lie down on a bed and go to sleep. She had sat in that brocade wing chair and yelled at everybody, especially Jimmie.

"It was fun getting this way, Jimmie!" she pounded the wing chair. "But it sure is *hell* now, you son of a bitch!"

"It sure is *hell,* Evelyn," he agreed.

Willy knew they never tried to get two kids on the same shot. Nobody with any sense would want to get two kids. She knew it was a brilliant cosmic mistake. But one they took credit for, nevertheless. After all, twins made you famous.

And these twins were the biggest and loudest and healthiest twins anybody had ever seen in Badin. Willy weighed seven pounds, and Kepley weighed six, but soon he caught up with her, overtook her, and stayed taller and heavier.

Bald-headed as two geese the day they were born in October, by the next summer, they had blond fuzz that thickened and got curly. Their eyes were gray, sometimes deepening toward blue if they wore certain colors. Or got excited about certain things.

Other than their blond hair and the color of their eyes, Kepley and Willy didn't look alike, shared no other resemblances than had they been born at different times and in different places. But because they were the first twins ever born in the Smith family in Badin, North Carolina, they were as odd as if they had been Siamese, celebrated and emphasized and insisted upon, *Look, it's them two Smith twins!*

Jimmie named Kep for himself, James Kepley Smith, Junior. So Evelyn responded by naming Willy for herself, Evelyn Willoughby Smith, Junior. And they went through Badin as Kep and Willy, the Smith twins, *two on one shot, two different kinds!*

Jimmie prided himself on achieving such a clever diversification. Evelyn was just damned glad to have them out, and to call her body her own again.

Long after they were old enough to be weaned, Evelyn continued to suckle them both at the same time. She sat in the big wing chair, and Kep and Willy sat, each with a nipple, sucking away and holding each other's hands. A cozy and blissful little group. And doomed to come to an end.

One day Orrie, grinning and gold-spangled, came in the house and saw them all three snuggled up in the chair, and she cackled and scolded, "Lorda mercy, Miss Evelyn, I mighta expected that titty-sucking keep going on with some people. But not with no nice people like you. Miss Evelyn, give them big younguns a Coca-Cola. Or a cigarette!"

Evelyn stared back cooly at Orrie. "I don't ever expect to do this sort of thing ever again. Not in my whole life. Not ever have another baby, or nothing. Not ever. So, I'm getting my money's worth, Orrie. Just getting my money's worth."

"Them two big younguns gonna bite your titty off," Orrie declared.

"Not likely, Orrie," said Evelyn. "Not likely." And she glared down on Willy and Kepley. "I'll kill the first one that bites."

Orrie grinned, waggled a finger, and went home to tell Bishop LeGrande, "She just like them big titties. That's why she keep on."

Orrie's scorn took effect. They were weaned, and Evelyn let her big titties dry up, never wanting to feel babies sucking on her again, having gotten, she was satisfied, her money's worth. Then Kepley and Willy sucked their thumbs. And if they were feeling especially generous, they exchanged thumbs, Willy's in Kep's mouth, and his in hers.

A snapshot from that time always bothered Willy. They sat on the front steps of the Badin house, both of them in little red-checked sunsuits, their feet in red sandals, their thumbs in each other's mouth, all eyes, all sucking bliss, all generosity. Because their thick blond hair drooped in curls from the summer heat, it was hard to tell which one was Kepley, which one was Willy.

Whenever Willy looked at the snapshot, as a child, and later as a grown woman suckling her own child, Shura, she always felt a curious stuck-together attraction of shame and delight. Evelyn snapped the picture because she thought it was funny, Willy and Kep sitting there, sucking each other's thumb, just another silly thing her twins got caught doing.

"You see that, Jimmie," she pointed out, waving the picture at him, "first I had to get them off the tit, now I've got to get them off the thumb, each other's thumb!"

"Well, Evelyn." He took the picture, studied it. "It's your fault for letting them hang on to your big tits for so long."

For Willy, the sensation inside the picture was the same half-frightening and half-comforting sensation that Bishop LeGrande and Orrie had always aroused. Orrie with those gold-spangled teeth, Orrie waggling her black fingers and grinning, trying to coax something out of Willy and Kep that Willy could not figure. And old Bishop just gazing and studying them both, finally pronouncing, "Ain't it sad the way life turns out."

It was the same half fright that turned Willy to develop teeth and sharp claws, and make up the wonderful dangerous and golden slanty-eyed Wolfsheena. The same half comfort that she felt looking at Marshall, forsaking her teeth and sharp claws, and accepting, instead, Marshall, his gold-spangled smile and his hard body and his trust.

Even more than tormenting Marshall, the safe man she married, the man who kept the edge, Willy loved tormenting Kep. Loving and tormenting. They slept together in the double bed because Evelyn was too lazy to separate them at first, and they ate and played, fought and scratched and bit. Their eyes lit up with secrets, little special jokes. Insular and conniving, they acted as a unit against the rest of Badin, against Evelyn and Jimmie, Bishop LeGrande and Orrie, anybody.

They had a cherishing and greedy and jealous love between them, a child's carnal bliss, pure and graceful as two pagans. Their playful incest in the double bed, silly and goofy and innocent, was another joke. It was a competition, a fight to get away with, and they didn't care where it led them, even when it frothed over in killing hate.

"I'll kill you, Willy," Kep threatened, punching her in the stomach.

"I'll kill you first." She yanked his thick hair. "I'll get you in trouble. I'll tell Mother on you, Kep."

They reached toward each other, somebody close enough to kick and bite, somebody you slept with, somebody to fight and make fun of, somebody to watch every day wake up with a heartbeat the same as you. Who *was* you.

They preserved a backward narcissism. Keeping it all in the family. Willy reached toward herself, backward, maybe, reaching toward Kepley. She didn't know what she wanted out of him, out of herself, even. Not yet, anyway, back in Badin in the double bed upstairs across the hall from Jimmie and Evelyn. She couldn't put a finger on it and name it, anymore than those curious stuck-together feelings of half fright, half comfort excited by the presence of Bishop and Orrie and the snapshot of her and Kepley sucking each other's thumb.

Willy really could pick herself out on the snapshot. She was the smaller twin. But just for a moment, squenching up her eyes, she looked like Kepley, and he looked like her, sitting there in Badin, North Carolina, thumb in mouth, suck, suck, drown.

Willy liked and hated it. She intended to kiss frogs into handsome princes, maybe frogs into beautiful princesses, all the same. And if she couldn't break their spell, she would kill them, stomp the frogs into bloody disgusting slime all over the sidewalk. She intended to figure out which twin she was, for sure, not according to size on a snapshot Evelyn Smith made by chance one hot summer when she didn't have anything else to do in Badin.

Willy meant to fix herself for sure according to name and definition, making sure she was more than half a person, part of a set, something thrown into the deal, Willoughby, Willy, *There goes that girl twin. They both got blond hair. Ain't that cute?*

Later, making love with Marshall Bell, Willy got both the prince and the gold, and things got stuck together into something bigger and more curious than she counted on. Things took on a shape that got sharper and more slanty-eyed by the hour. With real teeth.

But before Marshall, Willy loved and tormented Kep, had bad dreams in Badin about Wolfsheena attacking Kepley while Orrie waggled her black fingers and scolded, "Now you oughta know better," and bright swords sliced the night in two bloody pieces.

The story about King Solomon slicing the baby scared her. "He wasn't really going to?" she asked their Sunday School teacher, Mrs. Crump. "Not really cut it in two pieces?"

"I don't know, Willoughby." Mrs. Crump pushed away her questions. She was annoyed by the things Willy asked. She called her Willoughby, too, and sometimes Willy liked that all right, and sometimes she complained.

"My name is Willy. Call me Willy," adding, "But it would bleed, if he cut it in two pieces. It would die!"

Mrs. Crump waved a hand at her, "Shh."

"God would save it, dummy," said Kepley. "God would go Pow! and one half of it would be a baby. And he would go Pow! and the other half of it would be a baby, too."

Kep rolled up his Sunday School booklet and honked through it. "Pow!," echoing, "Dummy!"

King Solomon didn't scare Kepley. He could just say Pow! and it would go on okay. Willy admired his superiority, and she wanted to be superior, too, be Kepley, everywhere and everything he was. She wanted to feel him roll over her when they tangled on the bed, or through the grass in the front yard, listen to his wild giggles deepen to growls way down inside his growing, hardening boy's body, feel him echoing and spreading all through her.

Willy liked to lie there in the grass, or in their bed, just the reverse of the way they had been inside Evelyn. She took a long time saying, "Okay, Kepley, get off. Let me up."

She could have lived forever in Badin, insular and conniving, sucking Evelyn's big tits in the wing chair, sucking thumbs on the steps, until King Solomon sliced through them, *Pow!* and one half was Willy, and *Pow!* the other half was Kep.

The plain daily circumstances of Badin separated them. First, Badin Elementary School. The teachers put them in different rooms. Willy hated it and cried for days, standing outside the first grade door while Evelyn threatened and Mrs. Crump cajoled. Then she got used to it, made friends, like Frances Murdoch.

"I want my own room," Willy told Evelyn, "Frances has her own room."

The sword sliced down clean. She and Kepley separated either side of the blade, Willy thought, his room full of Army surplus and model airplanes, hers full of gold teeth and black waggling fingers and Wolfsheena.

Evelyn even stopped dressing them up alike except on Easter. On Easter they appeared in matching outfits made by Grandmother Smith. She made all their clothes, until Kep demanded fly-fronts. Again, he made the choice, just like getting born, superior and all-knowing.

"I want a zipper in the front of my pants," he said, "not elastic, like girls. I want a zipper."

And Kepley got a zipper, and they were separated all the more on the surface. The secret union, with its jokes and its charm, continued, though. Willy's old love-hate obsession kept right on.

Another snapshot proved it. That one, a near blur, caught them in a little spiral cloud, all eyes and arms and long smears of blond hair and white spirea blossoms. Dressed up for Easter, they posed again on the front steps, their figures defined by the big spirea bush newly blossomed.

Willy was proud of her blue dress, its full skirt like another blossom, ringed three times in lace the same shade of blue, and flared over a stiff crinoline.

"You can't sew a straight stitch, Evelyn," Grandmother Smith had reminded as she had every Easter since Willy and Kep were born.

"So it's up to me to dress these kids. Look, here, Evelyn, at this simple, and I mean *simple,* Butterick pattern."

She smacked the pattern on the kitchen table, scattering threads and scraps. "If you had any mind, Evelyn, you could follow this simple Butterick pattern and make Willy an Easter dress."

Evelyn smoothed back her own blond hair. "I did not have these kids to learn how to sew. It makes me nervous to cut out stuff and thread the machine. You do it. I don't care."

Evelyn looked at Willy fingering the soft blue cloth Grandmother Smith had spread over the table. "And, anyhow, Willy'd rather you did it."

Grandmother Smith made her a luscious blue dress. And she didn't neglect Kepley, either. In the snapshot, he stood beside Willy, crisp and neat in dark short trousers and a pinstripe jacket, bow tie, and long kneesocks as white and pert as hers. They were two beautiful Easter creations.

And as they preened in the sun, Evelyn framed and snapped them, burning them forever into the gut of her Brownie Kodak. Their memory got stitched together as simply as a Butterick pattern. And although blurred, the picture held together okay, diploid, haploid.

In this picture, Kep and Willy sat down on the steps, Willy on the left and Kep on the right, and his pinstripe jacket is somehow off, and her blond hair has somehow got loose, and their arms are reaching out in a near embrace.

Their faces, turning in a slow dreamy curve, have the wavering look of faces in twilight, or early dawn, or the blurring scary look of faces underwater. That time, or that look, in which nothing takes on a sharp focus just yet.

Their eyes look demure, looking down toward their laps, yet their faces are fiercely determined. They both know there is something they have got to do. And their lips are half opened, as though they just kissed.

Everywhere float fuzzy white spirea petals.

It was a strange moment. Like sleepwalking. Hypnosis. The real moment back in Badin that Easter rose and ripened, withered and fell away, all used up. But the memory blurred on forever, persistent and disturbing.

Evelyn said the picture was ruined, a wasted shot. "Out of every roll, there's always one," she complained.

"At least it was just one. But you know, Jimmie." She spread the little glossy prints in a fan across the soda fountain. "Some of these are good enough to get enlarged."

The big black blades of the ceiling fans swooshed overhead, and the smell of vanilla and menthol spread through the drugstore. Willy and Kep twirled on the stools.

Evelyn chose the shots of them smiling broadly into the Brownie Kodak, those where they both stood with every pinstripe and every thread of blue lace locked into perfect focus.

The one of them holding an Easter basket between them, she had enlarged and transferred onto cardboard, tinted and mounted like a statuette. Willy and Kep posed for years holding that basket on Evelyn's dressing table in Badin, smiling, gathering dust.

Perfect. Her money's worth.

FAMILY WOMEN

Push swing. Push swing.

A clumsy contraption.

The kind suspended on four white ropes and she sat on a glossy red wooden thing like a scooter between. Except the handlebars were lower than a scooter and it had a seat and a place to push with both her feet. She drew her knees up on the backward arc, then thrust forward, and the thing glided higher until it almost flattened out with her in the middle of it, went almost to the porch ceiling.

Claude Anne.

Somebody out in the yard said her name. Again, *Claude Anne. Why'd you all name that child that?*

Her dark hair, flattened in long braids with a few little wisps shabbying out, lifted off her neck, settled back again softly. Claude Anne liked it doing that. Like bird wings, she thought, my old hair is like bird wings. She pumped harder, the ropes squeaked and she smelled how new they were, smelled the sawdust still in the holes where the ropes went through, smelled the glossy red paint all over the slick seat and handlebars, the wooden pedals.

That morning, the first time Claude Anne saw the swing, she thought for a minute it was something for a sick person, a person with a broken leg, hanging down from the side porch ceiling, swaying gently in the March breezes. She thought it was what you put a person into in the hospital and hoisted up his legs and arms wrapped like white mummies and left him suspended there until he got well.

"That's your new swing," they nudged at her with their big grins and big hands, the family women.

She stood on the doorsill, twisting her braids, and studied it. "That don't look like no swing."

"Well, it is," her mother slipped around Claude Anne and pushed the swing back and forth. "You sit down and push it with your feet. Come on, do it."

Claude Anne got in, reluctant to undertake it with all of them grinning at her and urging her, her mother and the family women. Her daddy, she noted, was already out in the yard with the family men smoking cigarettes and fixing the oysters, drinking liquor straight from the bottle.

"I want a swing hanging out of a tree," she pushed at the wooden pedals and the swing took off, gathered force, and she thrust harder, all the ropes squeaking with such force her mother stumbled back. "Outside hanging out of a tree."

"Don't go so high, Claude Anne," she scolded, "this is for the inside, for the porch. You can swing when it's raining. This is better."

Claude Anne ignored everything her mother was saying, the agreeable murmurs of the women. She watched her daddy and the family men sacking up fresh oysters, hosing the sacks, then spreading them over coals in the brick barbecue pit, raising up pungent steam and smoke.

A big cherry tree stood about six feet off from the barbecue pit. Strong black branches low enough to hang a good swing. A swing with two ropes and a plank. That's what I wanted, Claude Anne assured herself, a plain swing hanging out of a tree out there with my daddy and the men and the oysters steaming like that and everything smelling like the beach. And smoking cigarettes. And drinking liquor straight out of the bottle.

Her daddy stood at the head of the group, holding his cigarette between thumb and finger, looking around at the rest of the men. She knew what he was thinking right then. He was thinking, I'm the best-looking man in this backyard, in this whole family. Claude Anne thrust the swing higher. She could see the spiders shrinking in the tongue-and-groove ceiling.

"Quit it!" Her mother stamped a foot. "You slow down before you hit the ceiling and bust something."

Claude Anne let the swing slow down, rocking, rocking, the new white ropes flexed, then hung taut as she sat there studying the family men in the yard. Her daddy flicked his cigarette stub into the barbecue pit, a smooth perfect arc, little sparks shuddering. I'm the best-looking thing on this side porch, she considered announcing to the family women watching her, I'm the best-looking thing in this family. And if I had a cigarette, I'd flick it just like he did right in front of your eyes.

Then she'd probably say, I love my Daddy more than I love you. And then they'd probably say, Did you hear that? Did you hear how sassy Claude Anne is? How hateful?

She wasn't an engaging or beautiful child, but a blunt and truthful one, dedicated and surefooted. She'd figured it out about the family. She knew something was bad wrong, that the family itself in a sense was *wrong*. But Claude Anne didn't understand what she'd figured out. Didn't know there was absolutely nothing she could do about any of it. The dark braids flew out behind her, then settled flat on her shoulders. Like bird wings, she thought again.

Then late afternoon, shadows like rich green oil spreading from under every tree and down the yard. Stronger breezes, with enough bite to remind her it wasn't that far from February. Claude Anne stood with the family men and watched them open the oysters with screwdrivers and knives, admired how they jabbed the hard shells and with a determined twist exposed the oysters inside. How they garnished the oysters with horseradish, ketchup, or plain apple vinegar and scooped the whole thing into their big mouths with saltines.

But she wouldn't eat a single oyster. She liked the way they looked, the edges curling, a delicate dark line around the pale glistening creatures. And loved the way they smelled. And the shells thrown in a pile beside the barbecue pit, pearly white inside, an occasional shimmer of purple, such loveliness rising out of thick rough gray ridges, this astounded Claude Anne. But she didn't want any oysters in her mouth, couldn't stand the thought of them going down her throat, sliding into her dark stomach and waddling in there, piling up in there, sticking together, growing thick in there like globs of snot.

It made her gag.

Oysters probably think awful stuff, she pondered, they feel awful things, too. Oysters know they're going to get piled up in sacks and roasted over my daddy's barbecue pit, something he does every year for the family, they know that and they hate it. Oysters can't get out of this. It's what oysters get done to them and they deserve it.

Her mother's laugh spilled out of the clump of women arranging things on the picnic table. There were no other children here. Claude Anne, at six, the only one. That family an unprolific group.

Claude Anne took a handful of saltines and daubed them with ketchup and imagined an oyster on each one. The taste was both sour and sweet, crumbly and salty, and left ketchup in both corners of her mouth.

"If you won't eat any oyster," her daddy bent over her, "you can't eat up all the crackers."

She smelled his wonderful liquor breath, a breath she thought was the breath of men, liquor and cigarettes and somewhere mellowing through, the smell of fresh oysters roasted in a sack over coals. She didn't open her eyes to look at him. Said, "These ain't your crackers. These is Mama's crackers."

There was a tiny silence, a moment when Claude Anne knew if she opened her eyes and looked up, she could see the hairs in her daddy's nose, see the flush invading his face, the fury. She could see his eyes just like hers, a clear Coca-Cola bottle green.

Then, "Mama didn't pay for these crackers," and he was gone.

The saltines and ketchup left in her mouth made a disgusting mess but she rolled it around and swallowed it down anyhow, then went to the picnic table for a glass of tea. Some of the family women were drinking beer in tall brown bottles and Claude Anne liked the way they did it, so accomplished, so certain. She wanted to drink beer that way. And bend over somebody and say, Mama didn't pay for these crackers.

She played and amused herself in the grass, growing chilly with the shadows, wishing for a companion, a little dog or something to run behind her. She waited to see if her daddy might join her mother around the table, under a tree, beside the barbecue pit, put an arm around her, draw her in to himself, maybe offer her a cigarette.

That didn't happen. Claude Anne sprawled backward in the grass and began to roll over and over down the yard, getting as drunk as she could off of grass sky grass sky smell of grass and black dirt and oysters and beer in tall brown bottles saltines ketchup and puke puke puke. And then she had everybody hanging around her, pounding her on the back, the whole family, her daddy accusing her mother, "Look at this! Can't you do anything about the way she carries on!"

Her mother flashing back at him, "The way *she* carries on! What about the way *you* carry on!"

And Claude Anne sprawled backward again, arms and legs like an X. X marks the spot, this is it, this is the place, X.

Saturday Night

Night screamed.

Claude Anne was so used to it, she never really woke up anymore. The night screamed around her, dark as a cave, resonant, lighting up in places like sparklers and showers, *Mama's having another nightmare.* Then long rumblings, *Daddy's tearing off in the car.*

This time she got up before anything started happening, before the night could catch enough breath to start screaming, before anybody could tear off in the car spraying gravel against the house. She got up quiet as death itself and slipped downstairs to the side porch where the swing hung gleaming in the moon, big moon, March moon. Claude Anne pulled up her nightgown and slid onto the seat, positioning her feet on the pedals. The glossy red paint felt cold to her bare butt and she shivered. The white ropes creaked and her braids slithered around her neck. And she began to swing, *push! pull! pull!* gaining speed and force, aiming for the tongue-and-groove ceiling.

Right overhead, right through the ceiling with tongues and grooves and spiders, through the sanded floor and the Oriental rugs, straight through the middle of their postered bed, the sounds of Claude Anne's belligerent swinging shot like arrows into the unsuspecting bodies of her daddy and mother.

They'll have to get up and come down here, she pulled her knees back into her chest, thrust them out full length, all the way downstairs and out here to the side porch and make me stop. The swing shot like a pendulum, the ropes eating into the ceiling, the glossy red paint chilling through her nightgown.

And if they don't come down here.

She'd swing until she couldn't breathe, until she slung herself through the ceiling and the sanded floors and Oriental rugs, until Claude Anne exploded up from the middle of their four posters and into the bodies of her daddy and mother. And then the night could scream. And then the car could tear off down the drive again, the gravel like little machine-gun bullets all over the side of the house.

"What in the confounded hell." Claude Anne smiled, pushed with such joy against the swing, pulled back with such assurance, she refused to stop at the sound of his voice. "Stop that! Get off that swing and back in bed where you're supposed to be!"

Her daddy barked like an old dog.

"This is my swing," she hissed, "this is my swing."

"I'll show you whose swing it is," he grabbed the white ropes and the force of her thrust dragged him across the porch floor a little space, then the swing slowed from his added weight, slowed and stopped and Claude Anne sat there waiting for him to hit her or holler at her something shameful.

She'd be ashamed. Not he.

"This is the very middle of the night," he added, steadying himself, justifying things.

But before he could do anything, Claude Anne jumped off the swing and vanished up the stairs, a glimmer of plain white cotton nightgown, dark braids snaking like whips, then nothing.

She knew down there he blinked a minute, gritted his teeth. *Claude Anne, damn little thing.*

She lay panting in bed, her heart thundering like the cattle stampedes she saw in cowboy movies. Clouds of dust, horns, cow faces, hooves stomping everything to death, and men riding around on panicked horses, everybody hollering, ropes circling.

Claude Anne turned over and buried her face in the bottom sheets. She could see through the mattress, through the sanded floor, down to the other end of the side porch, the place where the Whirlpool washing machine and dryer stood and the shelves with lemon-scented Clorox and Fab, the opposite end from the swing, the tools and gardening things. And her daddy still hanging on to the ropes, wondering what she was doing down there in the very middle of the goddamned night, *Claude Anne.*

Somebody's got to explain it all to him, she mused. She hoped he wouldn't come upstairs and ask her. In the next room, she could hear her mother already gathering up the strength to scream. *Take a Valium,* the family women recommended, *take a Seconal.*

It didn't matter. Valium, Seconal, Claude Anne listened to the night scream over and over. She knew exactly how her mother looked, sitting straight up in bed, the sheets like twisted lumps of laundry in her lap, her eyes staring and slightly bulging.

Then his footsteps taking the stairs two at a time, "Goddamn it," he pushed open the door, "if it's not one of you, it's the other."

He stormed around the room, kicking furniture, turning on lamps. Claude Anne's mother collapsed back into the pillows. "Oh, shut up," she said, a hand across her eyes, "turn out the lights."

Then his footsteps down the stairs again, the front door slamming, and Claude Anne, her face still pressed into the bottom sheet, her eyes burning through the mattress, watched the car tear off down the drive, watched the moon illuminate each little gravel striking the side of the house.

"Mama didn't pay for this house," she mouthed into the sheet, then turned and welcomed the sudden smack of cool air against her hot face. "Mama didn't pay for this nightmare she's having."

Sunday Morning

The walls and ceiling collapsed, the floor socked her under the chin, and when Claude Anne opened her eyes, everything started spinning. Vertigo. She shut her eyes hard again, buried her head in the pillow, Stop it! Stop it! And in a minute, it stopped and she got up cautiously and went downstairs in her nightgown.

In the kitchen, her mother was so ill-tempered, Claude Anne couldn't say a word or do a thing without getting glared at, so she took a bowl of Cheerios and kicked open the back screen and wandered down the wet yard. She paused to study the piles of oyster shells beside the black barbecue pit. They had heavy dew all over them and glittered in the sun that flooded through the trees and washed down the sides of the house.

Claude Anne nudged the shells with her big toe. She came out here without any shoes on. Her mother would have a fit, *Don't you know the morning dew will infect any cuts or scratches or mosquito bites you've got? Don't you know it'll get in through your cuts and scratches and mosquito bites and get in your bloodstream and go straight to your heart? Don't you know that, dumb little Claude Anne, huh?*

Claude Anne would like the morning dew to infect her cuts and scratches and mosquito bites. She would relish it passing through her skin and getting into her bloodstream and going straight to her heart. She nudged the oyster shells again and they tumbled over, reflecting pearly white, nacreous purple, and she liked it all the more. Morning dew and oysters infecting her, getting in her bloodstream, going straight to her heart.

Then her blood would slime up. Then her heart would glow pearly and blue in her veins, slowing down right below the skin. Claude Anne turned over a wrist and studied the blue threads,

Y's, they made Y's. The blue Y's flexed as she spooned the soggy Cheerios.

The pleasant ring of the telephone floated from the house. The family women calling her mother. *Of course, he's gone off, I can't stand it, I wake up and he's gone off, I don't know where, he does this to me all the time.*

Claude Anne dumped the rest of the Cheerios in the black barbecue pit, placed the spoon neatly in the bowl on the pile of oyster shells, and sat down in the wet grass. It spread through her cotton nightgown. *Grass stains! you know that's the hardest thing to get out, grass stains, and blood, you know better than this, I'll kill myself trying to get this out.*

The family women would comfort Claude Anne's mother, *Soak it in borax, honey, use 20-Mule Team,* and Claude Anne's nightgown would soak in the sink overnight, the green splotches slowly bleaching away, but not completely. Claude Anne would still find a faint greenish-yellow blur in the cotton, a place she could pull to her nose and smell, not 20-Mule Team, but the backyard and the morning dew, taste things infecting her, spreading through her bloodstream straight to her heart.

None of which was happening right then. Right then her mother complained and cried over the telephone to the family women and they soothed her and made excuses for Claude Anne's daddy, promising her mother he'd come back in a minute, *okay?*

They didn't know nothing, Claude Anne congratulated herself. All their power put together in a bowl of Cheerios wouldn't equal a drop of hers. They wanted to make him come back in a minute and say where he'd been. They wanted to make him stand up and confess murders like they were Perry Mason on television. They wanted to make him call Claude Anne's mother on the telephone and say he was sorry.

But that wasn't the way he'd ever do it.

I want to make him come in here and put his arm around her, pull her up close to him, close to the smell of cigarettes and liquor straight from the bottle, close to the oysters and ketchup. That's what I want to make him do.

Instead of making anybody do anything, Claude Anne went to the side porch where the swing was. Today it looked to her like an old-fashioned baby stroller hanging there, one of those things the family women called a kiddie car, not the plain swing she'd wanted with a plank for a seat and two ropes hanging out of a tree in the yard. Why'd they go to so much trouble for something she didn't want in the first place?

She mounted, the wet nightgown slapping her butt, and pushed off. They got this kind of swing, she sneered, because they probably saw it in a magazine. The idea made her so mad, she put down a foot for drag and stopped pumping. Yeah, they saw this in a magazine with a little kid riding and some mamas and daddies laughing and they got the idea to fix it for me on this side porch. They told her mother, *Now you get this and make him put it up on the side porch for Claude Anne.*

It was the way the family women keep her a little kid. Like the dark braids down her back. When all her friends were getting Toni Home Permanents or ducktails for the first grade, Claude Anne still suffered these braids. She was six years old. She needed a Toni Home Permanent, something dry and frizzed, something that didn't mean so much. These braids meant too much. They called attention to themselves and said, Look here, somebody really goes to a lot of trouble over this kid. Somebody braids her hair every day of her life. Somebody wants it to look special, every hair on her head, every inch of her body.

Claude Anne scratched a bare toe along the porch decking. I don't care if I get a splinter. I hope I get a splinter. A quick pain clawed under the skin and she flinched. I don't care. I'm Claude Anne by myself out here and I can take care of stuff by myself.

She remembered the family women teasing her mother and daddy, *Too lazy to think up a name for that youngun, so you all just named her for yourself.* She remembered her mother and daddy laughing back at them, agreeing, *Well, what of it? It suits her, doesn't it? Look at her. She's a Claude Anne if there ever was one.*

Claude Anne.

Too lazy name to think up my name. The family women teased about it all the time, *So lazy, so cute.* With this thought, Claude Anne pulled her hurt foot back under her, tucked it in like a doll, and felt dopey and sick because she herself thinks it's lazy and cute, what her mother and daddy did to her. She herself always plays the game and sides with her mother and daddy when the family women teased. *Shut up, I'm a Claude Anne if there ever was one.*

No.

Now she saw it was a different game. Something requiring grim and perilous measures, the simplest brutality. Something within her powers.

She slid off the clumsy swing, ignoring her toe with the splinter that throbbed as big as a balloon, and she plundered through the tools and gardening things on the porch until she found a pair of loppers. Then as easily as her daddy and the family men had pried open the oysters, Claude Anne lopped down the swing, sawing at the new white ropes first, then bringing it down like a big wounded spider. And when she had it all around her, the white ropes dropped over the glossy red body, she kissed the blades of the loppers and sniffed their old stale smell of green limbs and leaves.

She saw herself boring holes in a wooden plank, tying knots in some of these ropes and throwing the ropes over a big limb in the cherry tree near the barbecue pit.

And then Claude Anne, her vandalism all around her, saw the cherry tree years later cut down with a smooth stump broad enough for her to stand on. She would be eighteen, nineteen, Claude Anne didn't know how old, but something like that, a grown person with breasts and her dark determined hair clipped close to her head, and she would put a foot on the stump and declare in a dispelling, cheerless, triumphant voice, This is where I had my swing once.

She gazed at the picture, the cold blades of the lopper against her lips, the smell of the old limbs and leaves still climbing through her nose and infecting her brain, infecting like morning dew, *Don't*

*you know it gets in your cuts and scratches and mosquito bites
and gets in your bloodstream and goes straight to your heart?*

The picture fascinated Claude Anne and she dropped the loppers
to lift up her throbbing toe and examine the little splinter sticking
there. It slid out more easily than she imagined, a bubble of red
filling the skin. Claude Anne relished the blood and the throb
in her toe. Nobody had to explain it. Nobody had to prove it.
Everything got in her bloodstream and went straight to her heart,
okay. I love my daddy more than I love you, she'd tell them. Me
and my daddy can tear off from here and smoke cigarettes together
and drink liquor straight from the bottle. I love my daddy more'n
I love you, and he don't love nothing.

Claude Anne tapped the red bubble on her big toe, gently, and
put the finger to her tongue. A dull rusty flavor spread like a film.
He don't love nothing, especially none of you old women.

And she gathered her clumsy vandalism, white ropes trailing
from both arms, and pushed through the screen door and made
for the living tree outside. In a minute, she knew her mother would
come hollering out of the kitchen.

CONSTANCE

This New Year's Day, no day for weddings or anniversaries, is cold and wild with a harsh clear rain clattering over the roof, wind and rain sharp enough to eat you to the bone. Constance Biles knows that well enough, already depressed and she mocks herself further, pointing out she's really nothing in this family, a genuine nobody. She doesn't even have a *Jewel* in her name like her cousins. Constance, no middle name, no Jewel anywhere. Just plain Constance Biles.

Her Aunt Jewel and Uncle Lonnie got married on New Year's Day fifty years ago, before any of the cousins or Constance were born, and here they stand, she observes, Jewel and Lonnie, in another January and another new year, waiting in a formal receiving line in the Fellowship Hall of the Badin United Methodist Church, shaking the cold, faintly soggy hands of people who have come to congratulate them and eat up the big cake.

Jewel and Lonnie Biles, two old travelers, childless and independent, are, she knows, the richest people in the family. Aunt Jewel used to teach the sixth grade and would knock your knuckles off with a wooden ruler if you so much as looked sideways. Constance knows. She had to go through the whole sixth grade with her. Aunt Jewel knocked off her knuckles every damn day. And today Constance can still feel a slight throb in the backs of her hands and for a moment looks around for anything shocking she might do later, anything, just daring the smack of the ruler.

Aunt Jewel wears yellow rosebuds on her shoulder. Jewel Ellen, the oldest of Constance's cousins, pinned the rosebuds on Jewel as soon as they got there, giggling and squeaking, "Aunt Jewel! You look like a celebrity! All you need is a mink!"

Constance hates the way Jewel Ellen squeaks. Like something waxed to a big bright patent leather shine. Like those black patent leather shoes kids wear. Mary Janes, their mamas called the shoes. And that is the irritating sound of Jewel Ellen's squeak. A genuine Mary Jane patent leather shine. We're grown-up women now, Constance sneers, and she still squeaks like a five-year-old. Every time I call her up, I never know exactly what I've got on the other end of the phone. She goes, Hello! Hello! in that silly squeaky breathless way.

Constance also hates the way she lets Jewel Ellen's voice get on her nerves. And she'd vowed right then to ignore it.

But right then Jewel Ellen pinned a yellow boutonniere on Uncle Lonnie, giggling and squeaking the same idiotic way, "Good-looking as you are, Aunt Jewel's going to get jealous!"

It makes Constance sick. It makes her want to kill Jewel Ellen.

Aunt Jewel wants to kill her, too, Constance recognizes with a degree of comfort. Aunt Jewel knows that squeaking fool was probably named after her just to try and get her money. This delights Constance. We're comrades, she blinks, Aunt Jewel and I. We can see through the family's little schemes.

Which isn't hard. Because this New Year's Day a bevy of name-sakes flocks to the Fellowship Hall: Mary Jewel and Jewel Ann and Linda Jewel and Jewel Lee. Constance's cousins. Just the thought of them, just having to call up all their ridiculous names, could be enough to kill both her and her old Aunt Jewel.

Constance watches Aunt Jewel grimace, straighten herself, adjust the yellow rosebuds on her shoulder and reach to grasp the next hand that comes down the line. Somewhere in the background, Jewel Ellen's squeaking blurs into the general convivial confusion.

Nobody ever named a child after Lonnie. Constance muses on this, watching him in the receiving line. They all zoomed in on Jewel, probably thinking she was the softie, the one who controlled the money, the one who could be flattered. It makes Constance want to guard old Uncle Lonnie, and congratulate him, too. Lonnie, she can see, probably hadn't realized there were so many people in Stanly County who would come out in this miserable weather for a slice of cake and a cup of lime punch.

Constance looks down in the punch bowl.

"What's this stuff?" Zackie Hatley has eased up beside her and stares down in it, too.

She pours Zackie a cup and he holds it in front of the candle flames. "What is it anyhow?"

The punch reflects a pale green wash over his thin freckled nose and cheeks.

"Pineapple juice and Kool-Aid," she says. "Maybe with some lime sherbet floating around, all mixed up."

Zackie drinks it down, licks his lips. "Tastes like dog puke."

"I don't know. I never drank dog puke," Constance says.

"You drank this. I saw you."

Zackie Hatley burned up the garage when they were eight years old. It was during the Second World War and everybody's daddy was gone off killing Japs and Germans and they were stuck in Badin with their mamas who were nervous and always getting a sick headache and hollering at them.

Zackie got the idea they'd burn up a pile of dry leaves and run jump over them to test how tough they were. The higher the fire, the more they had to jump and the tougher they were. This was wonderful except Zackie didn't pay any attention to the leaves catching fire to more dry leaves and then licking up a few dead hollyhocks beside the garage and then catching the garage on fire, too. The car was inside, a shiny maroon Packard. It burned up with the garage.

Zackie and Constance hid in the ditch. Their mamas and the neighbors ran out and screamed and called the fire department, which was nothing but a few old guys too old to go to war. They sprayed the garage but it was too far gone. Their mamas cried. They thought Zackie Hatley and Constance Biles were burning up in the garage, too. That made them want to hide in the ditch forever. They didn't care that they burned up the garage and the maroon Packard. But it bothered them to make their nervous mamas think they'd burned up, too.

They stayed in the ditch until Jewel Ellen, Zackie's big sister, spotted them. "There they are!" she squeaked and jumped in the ditch and hauled out Zackie by his collar.

Their mamas started screaming all over again, kissing them, patting their arms and legs, then they beat the hell out of them both.

"You burned up the car in the garage!" they said. "All that gasoline! All those rubber tires! What do you mean burning up the damn car?"

And they cuffed Zackie and yanked Constance's hair. Jewel Ellen stood there with her arms folded. "They oughta been burned up, too," she squeaked.

"Shut up," the mamas turned on Jewel Ellen then. "Don't say that. How can you say a thing like that!"

Jewel Ellen stalked off. She had long tanned legs Constance envied back then. "Well, it's the truth," she squeaked, slamming the porch screen.

Zackie and Constance had taken some comfort in the fact that although their mamas beat the hell out of them, they honestly didn't want them to get burned up.

But Jewel Ellen's betrayal was bitter. And this New Year's, finding herself still angry about that betrayal, Constance looks around for Jewel Ellen and sees she is stuck in a corner of the Fellowship Hall with her fat husband Lex and three fat kids. Her legs, though, still appear to be long and tanned.

Zackie Hatley has married and divorced three times and that makes him something of a scandal in the family. "Nobody in the family gets married and divorced three times," Constance often points out to him. "One time, maybe. But if you can't pick out women any better than that, you ought to stop."

"Well, I can't stop," declares Zackie.

Zackie's first wife, Rhonda, was named after the movie star Rhonda Fleming who had long red hair and plucked arched brows and wore strapless green satin dresses bunching up her bosoms and was always in pretentious movies with pirates and Indians and wounded men in uniforms.

Zackie's Rhonda had fuzzy brown hair and no bosoms at all to speak of and rarely plucked her brows in an arch. Tall and skinny, wearing her socks rolled down past her anklebones and popping bubble gum, she married Zackie the day they graduated from high school. Then left him in six months for a guitar-player who wore blue satin shirts and effected the look of Elvis.

That didn't faze Zackie Hatley, Constance thinks. Within a year, he was running around with Pam, a cabaret singer from Charlotte specializing in Cole Porter. And Pam charmed everybody in the family, including Aunt Jewel.

"You heard her sing yet?" she'd asked Constance.

"No," Constance snapped at Aunt Jewel, "I don't go hear people singing, especially people singing around Zackie Hatley."

Aunt Jewel sniffed, stirred her coffee, went on as if Constance said nothing. "Pam sings good. Zackie Hatley's got somebody now who will stick with him."

When Constance didn't respond right away, she elaborated, "Pam might even sing in the church."

"Zackie Hatley wouldn't be caught dead in a church," Constance contradicted.

"That's what I mean," she said, "a good influence. He needs a good influence."

Pam didn't sing in the Badin United Methodist Church. She told Zackie one day that what he did for a living was boring and she couldn't stand it. Zackie ran a radio station, WURS, a small affiliate stringing along with the bigger networks in Charlotte and Columbia. They gave a five-minute news-weather-sports roundup on the hour, advertised a lot of supermarkets and sporting-goods stores, and the rest of the time played music. Pam was right: boring. Constance agreed.

Cabaret Pam packed up and flew to New York and Zackie never heard from her again. He played Cole Porter stuff for weeks on WURS, then switched to Patsy Cline. Constance didn't think he suffered too much.

Wife number three was Constance's favorite. Eden, a gym teacher from Rock Hill, South Carolina, Eden had Zackie running five miles before breakfast, pressing his own weight, and learning a decent crawl in the Clorox-smelling waters of Mecklenburg pools.

She got him off Winstons and Budweisers and onto wheat germ and Charles Hoffman Hi-Proteen powder. Zackie Hatley started looking a little better, almost handsome, though there was always something suspicious about Zackie's good health, like he didn't mean it. The freckles, for instance, kept a sort of stubborn offended inflamed color.

And Zackie didn't mean it. His good health was a ruse to catch Eden. After awhile he quit running and swimming, too lazy to keep a woman like her.

Eden's long tanned legs made Jewel Ellen's look inferior. That was her downfall. Jewel Ellen kept on about having a baby, having a baby, and Eden wasn't having a baby. Jewel Ellen by that time had three fat babies.

Eden suggested Jewel Ellen put them on diets because of high cholesterol in children. "Your old man could stand to lose a few, too," she pointed out. "Look at him. He's going to die."

Lex lay around on the couch looking at television all the time. "He makes money," said Jewel Ellen, "Lex works hard all day making money. Anybody who makes as much money as Lex deserves to lay around if he wants."

She drew herself up like the Statue of Liberty and lifted an arm. Jewel Ellen would fight for fat old Lex on the couch looking at Wheel of Fortune. Constance happened to be in the kitchen opening a bag of Cheetos for the fat babies and fat Lex. Zackie was sprawled in the den, too.

"Well," Eden arched her brows, "you can bury them all in big orange bags." And she walked out of Jewel Ellen's house and out of Zackie Hatley's life at the same time.

She was the only one of his wives Constance tried to get to stay. "Don't go," she said, "you're the best thing ever happened to Zackie, to the whole family."

Eden was stuffing gym clothes in a big shiny nylon bag. It seemed everything she had was Lycra and piles of pastel running shoes all light as bird bones. "I give up on this family, Constance," she said. "Even you."

"Why me?" Constance was hurt. She liked Eden and there Eden was giving up on her like she didn't count any more than Jewel Ellen or Zackie. Or big fat Lex.

Eden fixed Constance with a hard look, "Because you don't do anything either."

"I'm not fat!" Constance protested. "I don't eat Cheetos. I'm not having a baby!"

"But you don't do anything," repeated Eden. "You just leave it like it is."

And here was Constance Biles, a whole year later, on New Year's Day helping celebrate Aunt Jewel's and Uncle Lonnie's golden wedding in the Badin United Methodist Church. A cold wet day. Constance Biles, still single, with no husband, no fat baby, not even a big orange bag. And, as she has already mocked herself, she's a nobody in this family, a nothing.

Not even a "Jewel" in the middle of her name.

Like Eden said, she didn't do anything.

So she decides to just skip the deal, turn her back on everything and go. Constance presents herself to say good-by. Aunt Jewel is hitching up her panty hose, taking advantage of the waning festivities.

"You got any cigarettes, Constance?" she asks. "I got a headache only a cigarette can knock out."

"I quit," Constance says, helping to smooth Aunt Jewel's skirt.

Aunt Jewel looks disgusted a minute, as if Constance had failed a test in the sixth grade. And again, Constance almost feels the tingle of the wooden ruler across her knuckles. So she hurries to add:

"I hope you have fifty more wedding days, Aunt Jewel!"

"Not with Lonnie," Aunt Jewel declares, "not with Lonnie."

Constance is just before protesting, offering some little ridiculous encouragement, just before patting Aunt Jewel on the back, saying something like, But you've been together all this time, why not fifty more?

Then she gazes at Uncle Lonnie across the hall dipping into the green punch, at freckled Zackie Hatley loitering there still running his mouth, sassy and dazzling, and at Jewel Ellen squeaking among the rest of the Cousin Jewels.

This is not Lonnie's fault, she wants to point out. This is like when we burned up the Packard and everybody thought we burned up, too, and then they beat the hell out of me and Zackie when we were okay. This is the way we are in this family, Aunt Jewel. This is what you get.

But before any of this, Aunt Jewel says, "Go ask Lonnie. Ask him if he wants fifty more."

"You don't mean that."

"Why not?" Aunt Jewel sounds downright combative. And Constance feels moved to defend the family, even all the Jewels out there milling around, even Zackie, everything and everybody, herself, too, alone and childless. Maybe it is something, after all, just to leave it as it is, despite what Eden said last year. Maybe it is something, even if Zackie can't pick women well enough to keep one married to him. Maybe it is something just to come together in a Methodist Fellowship Hall on a cold wet New Year's Day.

It's the family, it's who we are.

And so she tells Aunt Jewel that, and then Constance watches Aunt Jewel smooth her dress again over the panty hose lines and straighten the yellow rosebuds. And right before Aunt Jewel can snap back an answer, Constance smiles as stubborn and sweet and mean as hell, and goes out the door of the Methodist Fellowship Hall where a fresh gust of January rain sharpens her color, inspires her vigor, and the parking lot is emptying, finally, of people coming to celebrate.

It's what you get, it's all you get.

EASTER HUNTING

My name is Coogan. People blink when they hear it.

My dead daddy's name, and also another name, Mary, which I
don't use anymore. My daddy burned up, crashed in World War II,
fighter pilot. I never even saw him. Mary Coogan, Mary Coogan,
that's what they called me at school, at Sunday School. Then I got
it stopped, and never knew I could until Dabney, my half sister,
told me. She knew things.

I stood in the middle of the Badin apartment, scrubbing my
sunburned feet into my mother's wine wool rug. She'd sent bags
of old skirts and sweaters and old snow suits to some mill in
Wisconsin. They were supposed to make a perfect wine rug out
of it. But when it came back and she spread it on the living-room
floor, she frowned and hooted and pestered.

"That's not my rug," she declared as my stepfather came in. He
tramped halfway across the living room before he even noticed
the wine rug.

"What damn rug?" He looked at her. She'd taken a position on
the couch right under her baroque oval mirror. Everything in that
room was centered, everything, and any place you stood or sat
had something hanging right in the middle of a wall or appointed
at either end of a piece of her floral furniture.

Dabney and I used to push things just a little bit out of line, just
enough to throw her off. "That damn rug," she nodded, "the one
you're standing on top of."

He looked down, blinked, then walked the rest of the way across
the wine wool. "Well," he said, "if it's not yours, then whose the
hell is it?"

He was already unfolding the paper, settling into his armchair, a rump-sprung, spraddled old creation he dearly loved, the only thing in the room without a floral slipcover jammed and puckered over it. He sat deeply, threw one leg over the side and dangled his foot as he turned the pages.

I liked this man fine. He was her third husband. The only daddy I ever knew. Dabney's real daddy lived in Asheville and she got on a Carolina Trailways bus every summer and went to see him up there. My mother didn't have any luck with men. Divorced Dabney's daddy. Let mine get killed by Germans and Japs. Then she married Ray. He worked in the generator room at the aluminum smelter, adjusting the turbines and stuff to keep huge jolts of electrical power surging through Badin Dam. All of which resulted in perfect metal ingots poured and cooled and shipped out of Badin to places where they got pressed into airplane wings, cooking pots, toothpaste tubes, and foil.

What Ray did for a living impressed me. Like taking on Marjorie Elder, my mother, with two growing girls. Like marrying into a bunch of aliens. No other children. Dabney and I were enough.

And here my mother was pestering this man, Ray, who controlled elemental forces and directed surges of electricity, she was pestering him with a damn wine wool rug.

"Get me a drink, somebody," he declared, and I went to the Kelvinator, slipping my sunburned feet against the linoleum. I got the cold fifth of Four Roses, poured a shot, added a tap-water chaser, and took it back to Ray on a little aluminum tray. My mother made that tray in her Home Demonstration Club, used black chemicals to etch the design into pure aluminum, a design of wheat garlands and leaves wavering across the luminous surface.

"You don't give a shit, do you, Ray?" But before Ray could say anything back, my mother suddenly gave it up, yawned widely, kicked off her flats, and stretched full length on the couch. "Oh, I don't give a shit myself. I don't care."

And she lay there staring up at our creamy ceiling, the Celotex panels carefully painted so no lines showed between them, no dark divisions marred the smooth effect my mother wanted up there over us.

I knew she'd given it up for the evening when she asked me to get her a drink, too, and I was glad. I got her drink, then padded upstairs where Dabney was sampling Tangee push-up lipsticks in front of our dressing-table mirror. This mirror was neither oval nor baroque like the one downstairs, but plain and round, not even a frame. But big enough to reflect us both.

I watched Dabney sample a fiery orange lipstick.

"What d'you think?" she paused, blotting her lips for me to inspect the color.

I liked it fine on her, but I'd probably never try it. Too weak, or too obvious. Me, not the Tangee. I either didn't do things, or I did too much. Dabney had no such problems. My half sister knew things. Weak, obvious, no matter. She knew, for example, the metal thing holding up a lamp shade was called a harp. It shocked me I didn't know that.

She knew, for example, three girls out at West Stanly High School named Blandina, Burmine, and Beautone.

"You just made that up."

"No," she said calmly, without a trace of argument, "they're cheerleaders. They're not even any kin to each other."

We started poking through her costume jewelry, big heavy stuff, bracelets and coat pins, clip-on earrings my mother called ear-bobs. Dabney was three years older than me. My mother, also her mother, married my daddy and changed Dabney's whole life. Mine, too.

I was jealous of Dabney's life before mine. I was jealous of her other daddy who lived in Asheville. Jealous of those special summer trips on the Carolina Trailways bus. Jealous of Dabney having my mother before I did. And she knew so many things.

"Blandina, Burmine, and Beautone," Dabney emphasized, holding a big pearl up to the light. The size of an acorn. "Anybody'd know that was fake," she said.

For a minute, I didn't know if she meant the pearl or the three girls out at West Stanly. Downstairs I could hear my mother and

Ray chuckling, amusing each other. The light was settling soft and easy over the apartment. Summer outside smelled like Coppertone and peaches. And inside it smelled like Dabney's fiery Tangee. And across Badin, past the boom and hiss of the smelter, past the dark glitter of Badin Lake, Ray's turbines and generators sucked electricity out of the water, forced it through the innards of Badin Dam and sent it zizzling back through the heavy cables to the smelter where it made aluminum all night.

A person could live a long time on such assurance.

But I had to grow up and leave such assurance and change my name from Mary Coogan to Coogan. Had to marry Buck Swann and go off with him to live in a North Carolina state park. Dabney thought I was crazy to marry somebody who lived in the woods. "You're a person who likes people around," she pointed out. "You'll get sick of nothing but woods."

"I won't get sick of Buck."

Dabney just smiled to herself. The way she used to in our round mirror, sampling lipsticks, telling me things she knew and I didn't. I hated her doing that. And she knew I did.

"You don't know anything," she added. She meant I didn't know anything about living in the woods, about Buck.

What did Dabney know about Buck Swann? What did my mother? A woman who'd had three husbands, divorced one, let another go off and get killed in a war, and then pestered the last one.

I shook the dust of Badin from my feet, big feet, size eleven, feet Buck liked okay on me, and I went with him to eastern North Carolina, a place of white sand and cypress, swamps and Spanish moss. My mother and my half sister never came down there to visit me. We wrote letters, talked on the phone.

Dabney was right about some parts, though. I didn't know anything about living in the woods, about the people down there around the state park Buck managed. It didn't matter to me for a while. Buck was enough. The woods closed in like thick green insulation, huge pines and miles of turkey oaks festooned in trailing gray moss. I liked to walk through the woods, then out along the public road, a hard-packed swatch of white sand that served as park boundary and fire trail.

People lived there, houses set far back from the road, and never took notice of me. But the Saturday before Easter, a little kid with a long black plastic gun charged me as I went down the sandy road, yelled "Get off this property!" her platinum hair flashing in the hot sun.

I'd never seen her out there before. And I hated her charging down at me across about a half acre of thick clover. Bees swarmed the clover blooms, and I hoped she'd get stung. It made me hate her more because she was a girl trying to kill me.

I blinked. Bright hair, platinum blond, that's what my mother's magazines called it, frowsed off her head like a curly cloud. Flushed with the effort of trying to kill me, she slid to one knee, took slow exaggerated aim. Then a woman hollered from the porch and the kid backed up the yard, still holding me at gunpoint. The woman waved, seemed embarrassed.

I stood there blinking a moment longer, then walked on, so mad I surprised myself. "Somebody tried to kill me. A little kid, a little blond-headed girl." I stared down at my big feet, hurrying to cover the rest of the road and get back to Buck. The sight of my big feet seemed to soothe me a bit. I liked the high-tops I wore, dingy white with blue and silver labels. I liked the heavy socks cuffed over. I liked the tan of my legs against the socks, and all of that put together, the size of my feet, the reassuring thud they made on the sand, improved my mind, returned me to what I wanted to do for Buck that morning.

"I'm going to dye us some eggs," I promised him, "all red, every one red like in this article I read in the *News & Observer.*" I had a big kettle of eggs boiling in the kitchen, and measured in some vinegar to clean the shells.

Buck laughed. He didn't care about dyeing Easter eggs. Didn't care about Easter or anything except himself, and me, the two of us right there in one place together without anybody else around to bother us.

"It's an old custom," I continued. "People in Czechoslovakia did it. Dyed all the eggs red."

"Why?" Buck slid one big arm into his uniform shirt, then the other, pulled everything up neatly and buttoned it. I watched a moment, absorbing the satisfaction of Buck in the uniform, the satisfaction of his body and his calm strength.

I used never to feel satisfaction. Although walking through the world and making claims on it, saying this and this and this, too, belongs to me, Coogan—I never felt satisfaction. Not until Buck Swann walked through and made a claim on me, without saying a word, or making a gesture, or giving one single haughty expression to his face.

"Say?" he pressed, "Why'd they dye all the eggs red?"

I smoothed my old jeans, sky blue faded toward cloudy. "Because it's the color of life. The color of blood. Because it's the only color they had, Buck. I don't know. I read it in the *News & Observer."*

And I eased around the kitchen table to huddle behind Buck and wrap myself around him. He felt big and serious in the uniform. The collar stood up crisp with starch from the laundry. Buck sent all his uniforms to a place in town where they did collars and sleeves good. He smelled good to me. Clean and strong and serious and big. The boiling eggs steamed and clattered on the stove, the vinegar almost intoxicating.

And now back from the sandy road, back from the kid and her big black gun, back in my quiet and secret kitchen, I dropped dye cubes into a bowl, poured in a cup of boiling water and stirred another tablespoon of white vinegar. Little red flares shot through the piquant bath, curled and clawed along the sides of the bowl, and then everything was still and hot and red, yet sort of fermented, and forceful as that vinegar stinging my nose.

I wiped off a boiled egg, balanced it a moment in my palm. I liked its smooth weight, still warm from the kettle. I liked how fragile it was. A thrust of my thumb and little fractures would web through it. I lowered the egg into the dye with a big spoon and listened to the pleasant little clunk it made against the bowl. A red Easter egg for Buck and me. I studied the egg wallowing slowly from pink to rose. A few more minutes. It settled on one side, turned to another, growing darker red. Blood red.

Somebody tried to kill me today, Buck, a little kid with a gun, a little kid with platinum blond hair, a goddamn girl tried to kill me. I am Coogan telling you this, Buck.

In half an hour, I had a dozen dark red eggs drying on the counter. They left blurry ovals on my tea towel, little pink and rose patterns. I hovered over the eggs, drinking in the smell, so piquant and close. When Buck came in for lunch, he said, "Hey, let's have a picnic at the goat house."

He started grabbing things and putting them in a paper bag, celery, carrots, the red eggs. "What goat house?" I added some Oreos and filled a thermos with milky coffee, stuffing in ice cubes and sugar, ice coffee for a picnic. "What goat house?"

"The goat house," he affirmed. "You'll like it."

An old run-down bungalow with sagging porches front and back, windows like sad dark eyes. But the thick grass was fragrant with explosions of rich yellow daffodils. I never saw daffodils as big and healthy and as blatantly yellow as those.

I touched a finger to them reverently. Pollen trembled on my skin. I held the finger to Buck. "See?"

He kissed it, sprawled back in the grass, cushioning his head on his arms. "You'll see the goat in a minute, maybe."

I looked back at the house. "What goat? You made that up, Buck. What goat?"

He took his time. "It's his house. It was condemned for the park. We helped the people move out. They got everything except the goat. He wouldn't leave and they couldn't catch him. So they just said to hell with him, left him. Sometimes he's looking in the windows. Big old goat. You'll see."

The smells of sun and clean skin, laundry and vinegar, lifted off Buck, along with a satisfyingly blunt smell of sweat. It was turning into a day of smells, I thought, March, early Easter that year.

"Why don't they come get him?"

Buck scoffed, turned in the grass to look at me, "Who'd come back to get a big old goat?"

Something in the way he scoffed and turned to look at me, something in the way he said *big old goat,* alarmed me. All that time I'd been thinking about a little goat, something pleasant and dainty, with white and brown patches and little hooves and curling horns, a little goat with a bell around his neck, a little thing to gambol and graze through those same big healthy daffodils I enjoyed.

People wouldn't leave a little goat like that behind. People would come back to get him. People would never leave without him in the first place. And there Buck was scoffing and looking at me and saying it was a big old goat. It made me remember, for the first time since it happened, the damn little kid trying to kill me that morning.

"Somebody tried to kill me this morning," I looked back at Buck just the way he'd looked at me. "A little kid with a gun."

"Where?" he sat up. I saw grass stains on the crisp gray uniform, and I grinned. I knew there was nothing Buck could say or do, nothing, because he had grass stains on his shirt, and I knew it and he didn't. And such petty considerations delighted me.

"On the road around the park, the old fire trail." And I told him the details of the kid charging down at me, telling me to get off the property, the woman interfering.

"That's just Jolene," Buck said, and lay back down in the grass. And he told me who the kid was and her mother and the whole history of the people living in the house abutted by a long length of clover and bees. Jolene's daddy, Buck said, worked as a smoke chaser, sometimes in the forestry tower, sometimes drove a truck for Bear Swamp State Park. "Just Jolene," he repeated.

And so there I was lying in a yard full of daffodils with Buck Swann, the yard so soaked from March rain the daffodil stems were taut with turgor. I wondered if either Buck or my half sister, Dabney, knew about turgor. I learned it in freshman biology. Swelling up with water. Or blood. Pressure against the cell membrane. But it's okay because the pressure comes from the contents of the cell itself. Nothing alien. It's your water, your blood, your daffodils.

Buck was cracking a red Easter egg, the dye coming off on his fingers like the daffodil pollen had come off on mine. And he was still talking about Jolene's people. "They're kin to the people who lived in this house, the goat house."

"Then why don't they come and get the goat, get it for Jolene?" I sneered, thinking of the platinum hair shaking over a big ugly goat, a mean satyr goat, a wild goat mean enough to knock Jolene down and hurt her. No more dainty hooves, no little bells. A big goat to chase Jolene all over the yard and knock her down.

I stood up then and taking a fistful of Oreos, approached the old bungalow. A dormer sagged right over the front porch, the tin roof scaly with rust. I circled the house, munching Oreos, thinking about how Jolene attacked me and how I'd love to watch a goat get after her. My bitterness impressed me. After all those hours, after dying the red eggs for Buck, I was still mad at an insignificant little girl.

I was mad, too, at Buck for dismissing her as "just Jolene," the same as he had dismissed the goat as "a big old goat." He was doing more than that: the way he said things and the way he looked at me, Buck was dismissing me, too.

I stopped, Oreo crumbs in my hand, chocolate crawling my tongue, and thought I heard hooves on the wooden steps. Thought I heard a quick exhalation of goat breath, a baaing. The big old goat will like me, I concluded, he will be tame for me. Let me touch him. And I turned, half hoping to look on the craggy, bearded face of Pan.

But the wise goat never showed up.

The next morning, Easter Sunday, a light dusting of snow whitened the park, unusual for March, not even that cold, and with warmer air aloft, it vanished by noon. Such delicate things. I looked at the white snow dusted around our pines and cypress, shivering down from the Spanish moss, and I realized I had an affinity for delicate things. And for violence.

The turkey oaks looked like gray toothpicks along my horizon, misty from the snow. I thought maybe women, or children, would suddenly come through the trees, out of the gray woods, like women and children out of the Middle Ages, like paintings you see of stark contrasts, medieval people struggling to eat and live and eat and live. The women and children would fade through the turkey oaks, then sharpen and color like a Polaroid picture for a second, then fade back. Like the delicate snow, appearing suddenly to whiten everything it touched, then vanishing by noon under a windy March sun.

I thought then I might get religion. Discover right there some strange image forming on my kitchen windows, go hysterical, see the devil or Jesus Christ. And I would tell the *News & Observer,* and they would write a feature, take pictures. People drive by to see it. It sharpens, colors. Then fades by noon.

All this while Buck poured coffee and fixed toast. "You can make egg salad out of these eggs," he suggested. "Or some goldenrod eggs."

"Goldenrod eggs?"

"You know, make a white sauce, mash the yolks through a sieve. Looks like goldenrod." Buck was grinning at me. "Like the weeds in the yard."

"I'm allergic," I grinned back. "I'm allergic to goldenrod eggs." The dyed eggs nestled in a little berry basket, leftovers, still red and vinegary.

"Well," he said, "you can go to the egg hunt at Lagoon this afternoon. Get rid of the eggs down there." And he was out the door and into his sleek park truck, vanished as smoothly as the surprise snow.

Easter at Lagoon Baptist Church was a ritual hunt for hard-boiled eggs in the turkey oaks across the sandy road, then dividing all the eggs among the children. Lagoon wasn't big enough to have real preaching on Sundays. Not even a real church, just a long shed with a steeple on top and six windows on either side, and a painted sign in the yard: *Lagoon Babtist Church.*

They spelled it the way it sounded, and somehow that made it more Baptist to me. Right away I saw Jolene at the bottom of the church steps waiting for the hunt to begin. Her bonnet, a crisp white straw, tied under her chin with navy ribbons. The crown was garlanded in little blue and pink flowers, their yellow stamens poking up like little yellow snake tongues, forked tongues. I saw Jolene brush the bonnet brim with her fingertips and flick the tip of her own tongue across her front teeth.

She must think she looks good, I sneered. The truth was she did. A smart pale yellow skirt of polished pique, a skirt with wide straps buttoned into a band, and a yellow bolero jacket made Jolene look good. And somebody had brushed her platinum hair until it frothed around the bonnet.

Jolene also looked as if she might kill somebody, hit somebody in the face with a boiled egg, kick somebody in the stomach. Jolene was the perfect combination of the delicate and the violent, and so I marveled at her until she hopped up, dragging her big plastic Easter basket, and said, "What you looking at?"

She had one of the few real Easter baskets I saw. Most of the kids came with brown paper bags from the grocery store. They had colored their boiled eggs with crayons, no hot dye, no vinegar. Their reds were crumbly Crayola wax. Nothing so smooth and dark as my reds glowing in a plainly woven berry basket.

I pointed at Jolene's. "You got a pretty Easter basket."

"Wal-Mart," she announced, "$9.95." And she totaled up for me the marshmallow peeps and chocolate bunnies, the thrush eggs and jelly beans still left in its bright pink grass.

"What you got?" she demanded.

I showed Jolene my red eggs. "All red?" she looked puzzled, almost sympathetic.

"Yeah, all red."

She waited a minute, scratching her knee. Then, "I want one of them old red eggs," she stuck a hand into my berry basket, chose what she thought was the prize, and plopped it into hers.

Now, my mother would've hated everything about Jolene, and about me even entertaining somebody like Jolene. And Dabney would've said, "What're you doing in a place like this, Mary Coogan?"

And then I would've had to say, "Don't call me Mary Coogan," and explain it was an egg hunt with real hard-boiled eggs hidden in the turkey oaks, and that these kids came out here with paper bags, except for a few like Jolene with gaudy baskets from Wal-Mart.

"Well, where's that man you married?" my mother would demand next, smoothing her hair sleek from the salon, yet envious of Jolene's platinum froth.

"He's off in the woods," I'd have to say, "working, and we're still married, Mama, not divorced. And he's still alive, not burned up in a goddamn war."

"But you still don't have any kids, Mary Coogan," she'd counter, thinking she had me good right then, just like Jolene yesterday, at gunpoint.

And right then, I hold out my berry basket, give her a dark red Easter egg, and one to Dabney, too. "That one's got your name on it, Mama," I point out to her. "And that one's got Dabney's. And all the rest of these," I cradle the basket to me, "all these say my name, say *Coogan.*"

It is such sweet assurance, such satisfaction.

The vanishing of all violence, the surprise of pure love.

And then my mother and my half sister, Dabney, fade into the turkey oaks like those medieval women I envisioned that Easter morning, and I am left with my name and all the enduring names of my children, *Coogan Buck Swann Coogan.*

POPEYE

Popeye looked good, grinning high over Brina as her kite climbed to the top of the scrubbed sky, a sky as blue as china plates, a sky pulled right up out of the middle of March, windy, sharp, the smell of spring behind every dip and bank of the atmosphere. Her hands got as cold and red as her face, all the feeling flooding as she rushed with the kite, giggling, calling out encouragements toward it.

Brina was forty years old, estranged, as they say, from her husband, sharing custody, as they say, of the kids. And as she ran across a green soccer field near the outskirts of town, a wide green space crowded by McDonald's and Harris-Teeter, she didn't care who saw. The damn kite was flying!

She'd put it together almost with disapproval, a fold of newspaper, the over-dyed Sunday funnies leaving colors on her hands. Glue, string, a rubber band to tighten the two sticks, and a tail of rags. *It won't even fly,* she thought, *I never got a kite to fly in my life.* Popeye came out on the underside of the fold, Brenda Starr and Dagwood on the top, some turns and crimps of the Katzenjammers, Little Orphan Annie, the Phantom, and Prince Valiant. If she squinched her eyes, Brina found it looked like a crazy quilt, a brittle patchwork of colors and speech balloons. An arrangement most pleasing to her sense of fate.

Get up! she encouraged it, *Hey, Popeye, sock Bluto in the jaw! Go on off to the Mystery Man in the middle of the ocean and find me something, bring me back something!* Pretentious little encouragements, she knew, but the kite flew, pleasing and surprising Brina even more than she'd first thought.

The first gusts took it up, wafting, vanquishing the stale smells of french fries, the oily smells of parked cars, their glossy hoods pinging in the noon sun. The kite went right up, tugging hard at Brina's hands, burning the string into her skin, *Hey! Wait!* People driving home from church, people rolling in line for Happy Meals, might be staring at her, pointing at her, but Brina didn't care, rushed on down the soccer field, encouraging the kite, *flying, flying!*

A silly thing. Her own kids were not even there to see. Nobody's kids were there, just Brina on the green grass, Popeye grinning and flexing his big muscles in the blue March sky. But Popeye looked good, *oh!,* but he looked *good!*

Brina, a made-up name. Her uncle came back from the army in France after World War II and told Frances Ann, her mama, his baby sister, to name Brina that. And Frances Ann, who didn't think through a lot of things, named her Brina Darnell Stubbs. Darnell for the movie star, Linda Darnell. Brina's daddy, a man who smelted aluminum for a living, sweating out his essential minerals and proteins and electrolytes on the graveyard shift, a man who stood in the hot showers of the washhouse a long time pondering the attitudes and positions of life, Brina's daddy scoffed, "Don't you think that's stuck up?"

Frances Ann considered. Then, "Anything'd sound stuck up with Stubbs," she decided. "This is different. This is French."

"Well," said Brina's daddy, "name her Dorothy Lamour, that's damn French enough, and a movie star, too."

"Don't be silly," she said, "this name is Brina, this name is from my brother in the Army."

That was forty years ago. Brina liked the name, liked the stories that went with it, her mama and daddy, the uncle from the army. The name, like the lost times with Quint, had once been a part of safety, a genuine shelter. But now Quint was gone with the kids. Frances Ann said, "The judge won't give the kids to Quint. The woman always gets the kids."

Frances Ann was wrong. They worked it out okay, at least for now. Still, Brina wished they were there to see the kite flying on

Sunday, not her weekend to have them. But they ought to be here, she argued, flying the kite was more important right then than what Quint did.

Quint. He made everything safe and silky for a long time. She and Quint both thought it would keep on being silky and safe. Foolish, foolish. They'd find the Black Orchid, the Black Pearl, that can of magic spinach, and a rich Daddy Warbucks.

But speaking of daddies, Brina's had dropped dead before she was sixteen, so it was just she and Frances Ann getting through everything, living comfortably enough on his pension, survivors' benefits, the smelter called it, nothing rich, no orchids, no pearls.

And then Quint appeared, coming back from Virginia to live in the house with his old daddy, Mr. Finger, living comfortably enough, two survivors, again, nothing rich, no orchids, and no pearls.

The facts of their existence ran through Brina's head, snapping as bright and crazy as the funny-paper kite. Quint making real leather shoes in his own shop downtown. Quint carving wooden novelties to relieve his tensions, to amuse her, the blade easing so quietly, so accurately through white pine, walnut, cedar. Quint taking her off to South Carolina to get married without Frances Ann or Mr. Finger getting to see it, to bless it or protest it.

And now Quint saying things weren't good, weren't silky or safe anymore. Saying he'd keep the two little boys, Emmett and Jake, in the house with him and Mr. Finger. Brina's two little boys, exceptional creatures, with her own whitey-blond hair clipped short and curling in cowlicks all over their heads, two little boys who tumbled around like little dogs and grinned and flourished, the flush of good health in their faces.

She missed everything. Missed Quint and the old house belonging to Mr. Finger, an oval of stained glass in the front door. Missed Emmett and Jake waking up in the mornings in that old house, spilling downstairs to slop Froot Loops over the kitchen and laugh at her and Quint and Mr. Finger.

Brina missed, too, the affectionate ways of Frances Ann, how she spoiled Emmett and Jake every time they went to her apartment.

Now it was just Brina and Frances Ann living together again, their old habits returning like old aches in joints and muscles.

The kite jumped overhead, and she flinched, expected it to crash, *Nothing's* going to last around here, anyhow, dammit. Not even a kite, not even a man.

Frances Ann had cried and carried on when Brina's daddy died. She kept pointing out things he could have done to stay alive. "He didn't have to keep on working in that smelter," she ran through it like a grocery list. "He could've got early retirement. He could've got a disability pension."

People brought over casseroles and pies in the hard driving rain all one Sunday. "He just keeled over!" exclaimed Frances Ann, as if he did it on purpose, "Just keeled over in the ingot yard!"

Maybe it might be better, Brina thought, up in her room, if he'd been run over by a car, or shot through the head. Maybe Frances Ann might be proud of that, take comfort in the violence of the thing. But to just keel over in the ingot yard?

She thought of her daddy keeling over, a hand to his chest, the surprise in his eyes—as his life passed before him. She thought how the noise and activity of the ingot yard went on, lights flashing, forklifts screeching. And then her daddy crumpled to the ground.

He was the first person she lost.

And at that time up in her room listening to Frances Ann below receiving casseroles and pies from the neighbors, Brina began to take stock of attitudes and positions in life as her daddy had once done. She noted the applications of fate. She grew sensitive to tone of voice.

Then Quint. The strongest, the quietest tone of voice. A man she wanted, an application of fate more dazzling than anything, including stars in the sky. He carried her off, like some vandal, some raider. But she was of age, no child bride, wearing a pink pique sundress Frances Ann made. A pink sundress Frances Ann had promised would show off her tan. And little did either of them know as the Singer machine whirred pink threads and scraps littered the floor that Quint would take her off and marry her in pink pique.

Then Emmett. Then Jake. Quint made little soft leather shoes for them, red leather, with tiny buckles. "You ought to get those things bronzed," said Frances Ann. "Put one on an ashtray."

"Nobody smokes anymore," said Brina.

"Put one on a picture stand, then," suggested Frances Ann. "Have Jake's picture in the middle, and his shoes on the sides. And do the same thing for Emmett's. And maybe an ashtray."

"Nobody smokes."

"Well, you don't know," said Frances Ann, "they might some-day."

But Brina kept the little red shoes wrapped in tissue after both boys learned to walk and tromped around in Keds. She liked to pull them out and hold them, rub her thumb over the soft pungent soles, finger the buckles. Then balance the shoes on her palm, such little things, both pairs on either palm, the sum total of her infant sons, Emmett and Jake, one on either palm.

Outside they could be killing each other, falling dead behind the lobelia bushes, resurrecting to shoot and kill again, *Pow!* Their hair glinted like hers, whitey-blond, except for those curly, tight cowlicks around their ears and over the crowns of their heads. Brina's hair had always been straight and thick, easy to brush and braid. Frances Ann used to braid it every morning in what she called French braids, starting with tufts high on either side of Brina's head, adding more, pulling them glossy and rich as platinum until they hung down her back, finished off with a gros-grain ribbon. And then she went off to school feeling slant-eyed from the pulling of that hair, feeling one eye might be higher than the other. The old days. The days of brushings and braids. Days almost silky and safe. Her daddy still smelting aluminum. Frances Ann still cooking bacon and eggs every morning in the cozy apartment.

She thought it could be like that forever. Going off to school feeling slant-eyed from the pull of love and pride, the faint smell of bacon in her hair. The plain routines of safety.

Emmett and Jake liked bacon. Brina fried up a whole package sometimes just for them, and Quint, and Mr. Finger, the strips draining into pungent curls on a paper towel. She poured orange juice. Made toast for Emmett and Jake to sop into their eggs, what they called "dip eggs," a plain fried egg, a regular sunny-side up.

And that, too, she thought would go on forever.

Then Quint said everything was wrong, they had to separate. "He's got a woman," declared Frances Ann. "They always got a woman when this happens."

So Brina asked, "Have you got a woman?"

Quint looked at her awhile. He was carving a giraffe for the boys, completing a whole Noah's Ark. The little horns on the giraffe struck Brina as being particularly delicate, precious, like her breath, the breath of Emmett and Jake, Quint, Mr. Finger, Frances Ann, even the breath of her long-dead daddy in the ingot yard.

"No," Quint said. He set the giraffe on the table between them, picked up the hippopotamus. Still a lump of wood, but Brina could see the animal coming out of it. She thought how it would be to have a little girl, to see what novelties Quint might carve for a little girl. A ballerina, some birds with long legs, a butterfly.

"Then what?" she asked, "if not a woman, what?"

Quint shaved the wood, coaxing and pressuring. "Nothing," he said, "nothing you did. Nothing I did. It's nothing."

Frances Ann said not to believe this. She said to fight Quint.

Brina pondered it. Quint, she knew, was not theatrical, not casual. If he said it was nothing, it was. If he said no woman, none. And if he said they had to separate awhile, even go to court over it, they did.

But fight him? Not believe him?

So she pondered more, as her daddy had done in the washhouse, hot water showering over him. As he had, possibly in the ingot yard, his essential heartbeat collapsing within. Brina pondered, grew sensitive to tone of voice, to irony and to silliness.

They shared Emmett and Jake. Quint spoke to Frances Ann when he brought them over. She spoke to Mr. Finger when she took them back. Everybody was so damn polite and noncommittal.

Emmett and Jake got in the bathtub, bubbles frothing all over, "You and Daddy don't like each other anymore," they did not ask, but calmly observed.

"Yes, we do," she protested.

"No," they continued, "you don't like each other anymore."

And the fragrance of the bath and the loveliness of her naked children combined to deepen her despair, cultivate her anger.

"They won't never get over this," said Frances Ann that night, Emmett and Jake asleep upstairs in Brina's old room, and went on to say how she blamed Quint.

"Shut up," said Brina, "it's none of your business."

"Well," Frances Ann folded her hands, "you better get something out of this. You better make Quint pay up."

"Shut up," Brina repeated. "I don't want anything out of this."

She hated the way Frances Ann made her feel, useless and dependent, like some sleeping beauty who couldn't wake herself up, a forty-year-old woman still waiting for a prince to come kiss her on the lips, a damn woman who couldn't find her way out of a paper bag.

Mama, she wanted to point out, you got something out of it, I reckon, when my daddy keeled over, you got a dead man's pension, survivors' benefits.

Mama, dammit, she wanted to impress severely upon Frances Ann, I don't want a dead man to pay for me, don't you get it?

And so on a lonely Sunday noon, getting the homemade clumsy funny-paper kite to fly, feeling it tug at her cold red hands and pull her across the soccer field, Brina hated and then loved with such a fierce pride, the knowledge nearly blinded her. Popeye dipped and pulled, winging like a demon spirit, his big muscles tattooed with little black anchors Brina couldn't even see anymore, but knew exactly where they soared. The people in the funny papers were distorted, exaggerated, played out beyond human dimensions. They got married and had babies looking like little moon creatures, big black eyes, red round mouths, speaking always in innocent exclamations, *Pow! Shazam!*

Nobody said dammit in Popeye or Annie, nobody said your husband's got a woman and it's his fault and you better get something out of this, you better make him pay up.

You don't believe Popeye. He's not real. Dip eggs are real, bacon is real, the touch of your children's shoes.

Brina grinned, wiped her nose on the back of her hand the way Emmett and Jake did, and thought how she'd tell them about this, the crazy kite she made herself out of practically nothing but the funny papers and it flew. She thought how they'd like it.

"Mama flew a kite!" they'd exclaim. "Got it up by herself!" they'd tell Quint, adding, "But first she had to make it, too." And when Quint asked, they'd eagerly detail the adventure, "Out of some old funny papers and some sticks and glue and a rubber band."

"And a long tail," one of them would remind the other, "a long, long tail out of old rags."

Brina blinked back her tears, glad for the sting of them, and, after one more proud gaze at its power, let go the kite. It sped away from her, a definite tingle returning to her cold hands, the sensation of little black anchors, little tattoos exciting her, *real, real!*

Acknowledgments

These stories have appeared, or will appear shortly, in the following places: *Crab Orchard Review, The Crescent Review, The Laurel Review, Negative Capability, New Virginia Review, Ploughshares, Shenandoah, The Texas Review.*

Some of the stories appeared in *La jupe espagnol,* Mare Nostrum Editions, Perpignan, 1990.

"Billy Goat" appeared in the anthology titled *That's What I Like About the South,* University of South Carolina Press, 1993.

I would like to thank the Glenn Grant Committee of Washington and Lee University for the generous grant that permitted me to develop this book.